"Can I make a suggestion?"

"You're the boss."

"I mean, just as me. Not your boss."

"Oh." Resting her hands in her lap, Lindsay gave him a curious look. "Go ahead."

"How 'bout if we both agree to let the past be in the past, and go on from here? That way you can stop apologizing for what happened years ago."

"Does that mean you forgive me?"

Until recently, Brian never would've thought that kind of thing was possible. But now, sitting here with the woman who'd single-handedly helped him save his fledgling business, he couldn't imagine anything else. Smiling, he said, "Yes, Lindsay, I forgive you."

She beamed at him. "If I could get out of this chair gracefully, I'd hug you."

"No problem. I'll settle for that smile."

"Really?"

"Sure. I always loved seeing you happy."

He hadn't intended to say that out loud, but when those incredible blue eyes brightened with joy, he decided maybe it hadn't been such a bad idea, after all.

Mia Ross loves great stories. She enjoys reading about fascinating people, long-ago times and exotic places. But only for a little while, because her reality is pretty sweet. Married to her college sweetheart, she's the proud mom of two amazing kids, whose schedules keep her hopping. Busy as she is, she can't imagine trading her life for anyone else's—and she has a pretty good imagination. You can visit her online at miaross.com.

Books by Mia Ross

Love Inspired

Liberty Creek

Mending the Widow's Heart
The Bachelor's Baby

Oaks Crossing

Her Small-Town Cowboy
Rescued by the Farmer
Hometown Holiday Reunion
Falling for the Single Mom

Barrett's Mill

Blue Ridge Reunion
Sugar Plum Season
Finding His Way Home
Loving the Country Boy

Visit the Author Profile page at Harlequin.com for more titles.

The Bachelor's Baby

Mia Ross

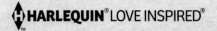

Recycling programs for this product may not exist in your area.

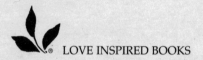

LOVE INSPIRED BOOKS

ISBN-13: 978-1-335-50933-8

The Bachelor's Baby

Copyright © 2018 by Andrea Chermak

www.Harlequin.com

Printed in U.S.A.

Love one another.
—*John* 13:34

For the talented artisans and craftspeople
working to keep our history alive.

Acknowledgments

To Melissa Endlich and the dedicated staff at
Love Inspired. These very talented folks help me
make my books everything they can be.

More thanks to the gang at Seekerville,
a great place to hang out online with readers—
and writers.

I've been blessed with a wonderful network
of supportive, encouraging family and friends.
You inspire me every day!

Chapter One

Liberty Creek was the last place on earth she wanted to be.

Lindsay Holland reluctantly dragged her feet up Main Street of the backwater New Hampshire village she'd escaped from five years ago, berating herself for allowing her life to slide so far out of control. As her mind took an unpleasant spiral down memory lane, she resolutely jerked her thoughts out of the past to focus on her immediate—and precarious—present. A long line of bad decisions had landed her here, she reminded herself sternly. Now she was completely out of options, and the only thing she could do was find a job so she could begin digging herself out of the black hole that had engulfed her and swallowed up what had once seemed to her like a promising future.

It was a frigid January morning, and a Monday to boot, neither of which did much to lift her mood. Pausing outside the only place in town that was currently hiring, she couldn't help smiling at the hand-lettered slab of cardboard hanging in the grimy window of Liberty Creek Forge.

"Office Help Wanted" it had said at one point. Apparently, things were getting more urgent, because someone had crossed out "Wanted" and in bold black marker had written "Desperately Needed."

Constructed in the 1820s by the founders of the town, the building and run-down cottage beside it didn't look as if they were capable of housing anything other than a lot of spiders and archaic ironworking equipment. But the ad that had been tacked to the bulletin board inside the post office was dated only two days ago, so she'd decided to take a chance on it.. How bad could it be? she mused as she knocked on the door. Worst case, they'd tell her she wasn't right for the job. She'd heard that so often recently, she'd become immune to the sting of being rejected. Almost.

But this time, she couldn't let that happen, she reminded herself. She had to make this work because this was the end of the line for her, and as hard as she'd tried, she hadn't been able to devise a plan B. So Lindsay squared her shoulders and did her best to think positive. It had been so long since anything good had happened to her, she'd almost forgotten what confidence felt like. How depressing.

When no one answered her knock, she inched the door open and realized that whoever was inside couldn't hear anything over the loud rock music and clanging of steel. She'd been on field trips to the old metal shop during middle school, and as she stepped inside and set down her single duffel bag, it struck her that the lobby probably hadn't changed a bit in the twenty-six years she'd been alive.

Neat but unapologetically functional, the bare-bones area held four mismatched folding chairs and a battered table that looked as if it could have been left behind by the original owners of the business. The stainless steel coffee maker on top of it looked decidedly out of place, and the collection of teas and coffees alongside it was an encouraging sign. Despite the rustic environment, it was clear that someone thought enough of their staff to provide them with some creature comforts.

A set of wide sliding doors stood at the rear of the entryway, and even though they were closed, she could hear the muffled hard-driving bass from a rock classic. Funny, she thought as she edged one of the doors open, it had been one of her favorite songs since high school. Unfortunately, that brought up more unpleasant memories, and she batted them aside as she strode into the production area of the metalworks.

As tidy as the front was, this section of the building was a step short of a disaster. A tall man wearing a protective mask and leather apron was welding one old piece of equipment to another, possibly even older, machine. Really, he should just call a scrap metal firm to haul everything out so he could start over. Then again, this was her prospective new boss, and in her situation she couldn't afford to be picky.

Before she could lose her nerve, Lindsay crossed the dusty floor and waited for an opportune moment to tap him on the shoulder. Clearly startled, he whipped around so fast, she had to dodge the glowing torch in his gloved hand.

"Oh, man," he muttered as he turned away and doused the flame. "I'm sorry."

He'd scared her half to death, but she forced a bright tone to avoid coming across like a baby. "No harm done. I'm pretty light on my feet."

For some reason, he kept his back to her and very carefully peeled off the gloves, setting them beside the torch before turning to her. And then, as if in slow motion, he swiveled the welder's mask back to reveal the very last person she'd expected to see today.

"Brian Calhoun?"

Framed by a riot of brown hair, his deep blue eyes narrowed in the expression she recalled only too well. Those chiseled features hadn't changed at all over the years, and his jaw clenched a bit before he nodded. "Lindsay."

"What are you doing here?" she demanded in a near panic, any thought of making a good first impression gone. There was no point in dancing around the issue. After what she'd done to him, she suspected that Brian wouldn't hire her if she was the only unemployed office manager left in the universe.

"I own this place," he informed her coolly. "What're *you* doing here?"

"Looking for a job," she blurted before reason kicked in to remind her that there wasn't much sense in pursuing this any further. Then again, it had been a long time since she'd left. It was possible that he'd forgiven her. "I was surprised to see your ad at the post office. My understanding was that it was more your grandfather's hobby shop than anything."

"It was. He had a heart attack four years ago and wasn't able to keep the place up the way he always did, so he closed it down. He died not long after that."

"I'm so sorry… I know how close you two were. You must really miss him."

"This was where he taught me about metalworking, so I decided to try running it as an actual business again. Kind of as a tribute to Granddad."

Having moved from pillar to post throughout her childhood, Lindsay couldn't relate to feeling that kind of connection to anywhere in particular. She'd never considered it a problem, but she'd been kicked around more than she would have liked, and now she envied him of those deep, stabilizing roots. Realizing she should say something, she searched for a response that wouldn't betray how dire her own circumstances were. "That's nice."

He didn't say anything to that, just stared at her with the penetrating gaze that had once fallen on her with such warmth, she'd almost believed that she deserved his affection. Now there was no sign of anything in it other than icy contempt, and after what she'd done, she couldn't blame him.

Just when she was about to concede defeat, the wording on his sign came to mind. She was pretty desperate herself, and while this situation was far from ideal, it was the only one available to her. So, hoping to appeal to the innate sense of chivalry that ran in the Calhoun boys' blood, she took a deep breath and summoned what was left of her dignity. "I need a job, and you need someone to handle the administrative end of the business. I worked as an office manager at a small law firm for two years. I'm very organized and will do whatever needs to be done out front so you can focus on production for your customers. I think we can help each other."

"Do you?" Cocking his head, he assessed her with a skeptical look. After a few long, uncomfortable moments, he asked, "How's Jeff?"

"Gone." She sighed, her fleeting bout of moxie evaporating like mist. "You were right about him."

Brian absorbed that, shaking his head in silent disapproval. Then, to her utter astonishment, he announced, "I always thought he was a snake. You're better off without him."

Bolstered by his reaction, she felt a flicker of hope that this awkward reunion might not end up being a complete disaster. "Thank you for saying that. I know I don't deserve it."

That got her a short, derisive laugh. "Because you dumped me for a sweet-talking loser who promised to take you to— Where was it?"

"Nevada. For the record, we never made it past Ohio."

"I'm not surprised."

Of course not, Lindsay thought morosely. No one was, except for her. Sadly, that had been only the first of many disappointments she'd had to contend with since breaking free of the confines of this Currier and Ives town to explore the world beyond New Hampshire. Her adventures had left her beyond penniless and anxious to find a safe haven that would allow her to gain her bearings and figure out what came next in a life that up until now had been dominated by wanderlust and chaos.

Working for Brian would be difficult, at best, but she really didn't see an alternative. "Past atrocious judgment aside, I'm an excellent worker and will do things however you want them done." Gulping down her anxiety, she added, "I really need this job, Brian. I promise, if you give me a chance, I'll be very professional and you won't have a bit of trouble with me."

He pinned her under an unforgiving scowl. "You let me down once. Why should I trust you again?"

"Because that was a long time ago, and I'm a different person now." He had no idea just how different, she added silently.

Another long pause. Conflicting emotions chased each other like thunderclouds through his eyes, and he seemed to be having some kind of internal debate about her. She wanted to squirm while he thought it over, but managed to stand her ground, holding his gaze with an unflinching one of her own. If he wanted to boot her out the door, fine. But she wasn't going to turn tail and slink away like a scolded hound. There was too much at stake for her to be timid now.

"I'm ready for a break," he finally said. "Let's go talk in the office."

It wasn't exactly the "you're hired" she'd been wishing for, but he hadn't thrown her out into the snow, either. Feeling more optimistic than she had in months, Lindsay tried not to get her hopes up as she followed him back through the shop and into the small office. The plate glass that used to separate it from the work area was gone, and in its place was a banged-up piece of plywood that had seen better days. Brian started up a space heater in the corner, and once he closed the door, the interior warmed up quickly.

"I'm parched," he said as he opened a countertop fridge and took out a bottle of iced tea. "I've got water, too. Would you like some?"

Considering his earlier comments, his offer of something to drink was a huge step in the right direction, and she nodded. "Thank you."

After handing her the bottle, he twisted the top off his and took a long swallow. She sipped hers and held it against her cheek, enjoying the coolness against her skin.

"It's pretty warm in here," he said, holding out his hand. "Can I take your coat?"

"No, thanks. I'm fine."

Her stoic comment earned her a chuckle. "Your face is getting redder by the second. If you're worried about it getting wrinkled, I can probably scare up a hanger for it."

"That's not necessary." Hearing the stiffness in her voice, she tried in vain to come up with a way to explain her odd behavior. Then, figuring that showing him was better than telling him, she set her water bottle down on the desk and took off her coat.

If she lived to be a hundred years old, she knew she'd never forget the look on his face.

"You're pregnant."

His surprise visitor shook long dark curls back over the shoulders of a maternity top that was better suited for fall than the middle of winter. Meeting his gaze with a directness that was a little unsettling, Lindsay gave him a pitying look. As they stared at each other, that all-too-familiar smirk crinkled the corner of her mouth. "Observant as ever, aren't you?"

Brian had no clue what else he could possibly say. While his brain was struggling to wrap itself around her stunning revelation, his hackles began to rise, and he fought to keep his voice down. "Is Jeff the baby's father?"

"Of course he is," she snapped, flinging her coat onto the cluttered desk in a fit of the flash-fire temper that had apparently not mellowed much over the years. After blowing out an exasperated breath, she faced him squarely, the spirit that had always captivated him glittering in those incredible sky blue eyes. "I was with him for almost six years. *Only* him," she added crisply.

Brian had a few choice words to say about the length of their noncommittal relationship, but he kept them to himself. At twenty-seven, he was a contented bachelor and far from being an expert on pregnancy. But he knew enough to be aware that upsetting her wouldn't be good for Lindsay or the innocent child she was carrying. Whatever had gone on since she broke his heart and left him behind, it apparently hadn't ended well. Piling on the guilt would only make her feel worse, and while the bitterness he felt toward his ex was still alive and well, browbeating her over mistakes she'd made in the past would be cruel.

"All right, I'm sorry." Motioning to the desk chair, he said, "Have a seat and let's start this conversation over again."

Her eyes narrowed suspiciously and she nailed him with a mistrustful glare. "You'll be nice?"

"Sure," he replied, doing his best to appear as if it didn't bother him that the troubled girl he'd once loved more than anything had unexpectedly dropped back into his life pregnant with another man's child.

"Promise?"

Some of the defiance left her expression, and he heard the slightest tremble in her soft voice. It made her sound vulnerable, like a frightened little girl who was searching for someone who would reassure her that everything was going to be okay. "Yeah, I promise."

In his memory, Brian flashed back to his junior year in high school, when Lindsay Holland had been the pretty new sophomore every guy wanted to date. One afternoon, he'd run across her sitting in the stands after a football game, crushed by the self-centered quarterback who'd just dumped her for a cheerleader. After comforting Lindsay, Brian had tracked down the arrogant jerk and made sure that he never forgot what breaking her trusting heart had cost him.

And now, they were together again, in more or less the same set of circumstances. Plus a baby, of course. The irony of the bizarre circle they'd made didn't escape Brian, and those old protective instincts kicked in, making him wonder where he might find Jeff Mortensen these days. "I never liked the guy, but I can't believe he'd leave you and his own child to fend for yourselves that way."

"He doesn't know about the baby. I found out I was pregnant shortly after he took off."

"Is that right?"

"I know that look, so don't even think about it," Lindsay warned, as if she'd read his mind somehow. "I don't want you getting into it with Jeff. We're not teenagers anymore, and you don't have to defend my honor. I got myself into this mess, and I'll come up with a way to get out of it. Eventually," she added glumly.

How she knew what he'd been thinking was beyond him, but Brian chalked it up to their shared history and the fact that he wasn't really all that complicated. So he shrugged it off and waited for her to get comfortable. Or as comfortable as a pregnant woman could in a straight-back wooden armchair. Once she was facing him, he started again.

Deciding humor was the best approach, he crossed his arms and leaned against the wall beside the beat-up table he used as a desk. "So, Lindsay, how've you been?"

Amusement twinkled in her eyes, and at last she smiled. "Good. And you?"

"Questioning my sanity ever since I came up with the idea of rehabbing this place and getting into the iron decor business."

"How's it going?"

"Nowhere," he admitted grimly. "I've got a few contracts, but the problem with specialty work is that once you've filled an order, there's no more coming in behind it. My cousin Jordan's planning to come help out once his summer season is over, which will make a huge difference in the range of products I can offer. The problem is, I'm nowhere near the artist he is, so I have to figure out how to keep from going bankrupt before then."

"Jordan, your cousin who does metalwork for the art fairs?" When he nodded, she said, "I remember him being really talented."

"He is, but his head for business is worse than mine. Which is why I need someone who's organized and good with computers."

Lindsay glanced around, angling to look behind filing cabinets that dated back to the turn of the twentieth century. Then she came back to him and grinned. "I don't see a computer."

"I don't even know what to buy," he confided with a deep sigh. "I'm a hands-on kinda guy. I can build or fix just about anything, but when it comes to technology…"

"You're clueless," she filled in, laughing lightly. "It takes a big man to admit he's got a weakness."

"You make that sound like a good thing."

All traces of humor left her features, and she said, "Being honest is. That's a very good thing."

Brian wanted to kick himself for making her sad, and then logic reminded him that he had nothing to do with the decisions she'd made that had landed her in her current situation. As she'd so readily admitted, it was her own fault.

But there was a tiny part of him, way back in the corner of his guarded heart, that still loved the girl she'd once been. The one who'd looked up at him like he was her hero because he'd stepped in to defend her when no one else would. Before she'd cast him aside for the hazy prospect of adventure, without an explanation or even a goodbye. "Lindsay, what happened?"

Instantly, she stiffened and glowered at him. "What do you mean?"

"I mean, you hated it here when we were in high school. When you left, I figured you'd never come back."

She hesitated, as if she was trying to decide whether to confide in him or not. Strangely enough, that was how he knew that whatever she finally told him would be the deep-down truth.

"Believe it or not, much as I detested this Podunk town, it's the only place I've ever lived where I felt like there were some people who actually cared about what happened to me. That's really important to me right now," she added, smoothing a hand over her stomach in a maternal gesture that struck a deep chord in him.

"I get you not wanting to be alone because of the baby, but why didn't you go to your mom?"

"We had a nasty falling-out, and I haven't seen or talked to her in years. I don't even know where she is, and if I did I wouldn't degrade myself by asking her for anything."

Brian vaguely remembered Vera Holland, a flirtatious single mother whose behavior had made life miserable for her daughter. Through no fault of her own, Lindsay's reputation had suffered, and more than once he'd spoken out in her defense when some classmate or another had assumed the worst of her.

Taking a deep breath, she went on in a calmer tone. "I've been living in Cleveland, and when it occurred to me to come back to New Hampshire, I found out that the newspaper over in Waterford has a website. In their real estate section I found a room to rent here in town. I sent the landlord first and last month's rent to hold the spot for me and then took the last of my cash to the bus depot."

"Let me guess. Jeff has the car."

"Took it," she clarified bitterly. "Along with all the money in our joint account. A few weeks ago, a collection agency called and, after some serious legwork, I found out that he's been running up the balances on the credit cards that were in both our names. The lawyer I used to work for helped me separate my finances from Jeff's, but my credit's shot, and the money's gone forever."

"But you must've been making decent money as an office manager. I don't understand how things got so bad."

"I was okay at first," she confirmed quietly. "Then I found out I was pregnant, and the stress I was under gave me some pretty serious health problems. Because of that, I couldn't work consistently, and even the temp agency stopped calling. The lease on the apartment was up, and there was no way I could make the payments, so I had to move out. When I left Cleveland, I had just enough in my wallet for the fare to Liberty Creek and a couple of sandwiches."

Trusting the wrong guy had all but ruined her life, Brian mused sadly. And now, her flair for poor choices and running away when things got tough had left her well and truly alone. Part of him still had a soft spot for the troubled girl he remembered all too vividly and was inclined to help her.

The other part—the smarter one—recognized that once again she'd fled from her problems without much thought about what she'd do when she reached her new destination. That had always been her MO, and apparently her tendency to dodge the hard stuff hadn't changed.

For all his wild ways, Brian knew he'd been blessed with a large, loving family that supported him no matter what he did. They'd even warmed up to his crazy idea of reopening the archaic blacksmith shop that had lain dormant for so long the equipment was caked with rust and bat droppings. Knowing that Lindsay was slogging through such a difficult time completely on her own made him sadder than anything ever had.

But he wasn't about to trust his fledgling business to someone who'd shown such poor judgment and was a proven flight risk. He had a large payment due on his business loan in just nine weeks. If the forge didn't start turning a profit soon, he'd have to stop his improvements halfway through and find another way to keep the place going. He knew that his family would contribute to the cause, but he didn't want to do it that way. Quite honestly, he'd rather sell everything he owned to pay the bank rather than beg for cash from anyone.

Thoughts of being strapped for funds prompted a sobering thought. "When did you last see a doctor?"

"About a month ago, when I was six months along. I'm not due until mid-March, and he said everything was fine."

But it wasn't fine now, Brian thought grimly. Anyone could see that. She was pale, and now that they weren't sparring with each other, he noticed the tired circles shadowing her eyes. Hopeful and hopeless at the same time, her cautious demeanor got to him in a way that he'd never experienced before. He barely resisted the urge to take her in his arms and reassure her, but he knew better than to let his guard down around her again.

Standing to put some distance between them, he picked up her coat and held it for her. "It's not a good day for walking anywhere. I'll give you a ride to that house you mentioned."

The hopelessness he'd picked up on finally won out, and she frowned. "You're not going to hire me, are you?"

He felt like a complete heel, but every alarm in his head was going off, and he couldn't ignore his instincts. "I really think it'd be better if I find someone else."

"Of course," she replied as if that was the result she'd been expecting all along. "I understand."

There was the professionalism she'd promised him, he mused as she slipped her well-worn coat back on. Calm and competent, it was the kind of temperament that he was looking for in the person he would be trusting to run his front office.

Crazy as it seemed, Lindsay would have been perfect for the job. The problem was, he just couldn't convince himself to trust her.

Chapter Two

Brian refused to let her carry her bag.

Lindsay couldn't remember the last time someone had helped her with anything, so seeing him with her oversize duffel slung over his shoulder did something funky to her stomach. Or maybe she was just hungry, she thought wryly. The effects of that stale candy bar she'd bought in Cleveland had worn off long before she reached Liberty Creek.

The town she'd vowed to leave in her rearview mirror, she recalled as they got into his big black four-by-four and headed to the address her new landlord had given her. Well, there was no help for that now. It was the dead of winter, and since she had no car, she was stuck here until the baby was born. After that, she could make some plans to move away, for good this time. Until then, she'd just have to figure out a way to make do.

The house wasn't far from the forge, in a nice, quiet neighborhood with a clear view of Liberty Creek's iconic covered bridge. She knocked on the front door of a small Colonial that was typical of the homes in this town that had come into existence shortly after the American Revolution. Tucked in for the winter behind wrought-iron fences that were almost invisible beneath the snow, many of the chimneys had smoke drifting lazily up from fireplaces that must keep things warm and cozy inside.

Family places, she thought with a pang of envy. Kitchens filled with home-baked cookies and pot roasts, the kinds of food that her own mother had never made because two waitressing jobs had left her with no energy by dinnertime. Lindsay remembered how her friends' moms had been—warm and kind, taking care of their husbands and kids every single day. She'd never met her own father, who'd bolted long before she came into the world.

Like Jeff.

More than once, she'd wondered if she was cursed to continue her mother's path of destruction in her own life. Pushing the gloomy thought aside, she plastered a smile on her face as footsteps sounded on the other side of the heavy door.

A petite woman slowly pulled it open and squinted out at Lindsay. "May I help you?"

"Hello, Mrs. Farrington. I'm Lindsay Holland," she explained, offering her hand and her friendliest smile. "We talked last week about your spare room, and I sent you a money order for the deposit. When I asked about moving in on Monday, you said that would be fine."

"And that's today?" the woman asked, seeming confused. When Lindsay nodded, she shook her head with a slight grimace. "I lose track sometimes. Please come in."

"Thank you."

The elderly woman gave Brian a quick once-over that settled on his boots. Grinning, he set Lindsay's bag down and said, "Don't worry. I'll stay on the mat."

"I'd appreciate that. All this ice and snow makes a mess of the wood floors."

"When I spoke to you on the phone, you said that you and your husband are from Georgia," Lindsay commented. "How are you liking New Hampshire?"

"It's cold and wet," a man's voice replied from an open archway that led into a living room that still sported its original wood paneling. He did the assessing thing, too, but while he instantly dismissed Brian, his gaze swept over Lindsay twice, and his jaw tightened. "May I take your coat, Miss Holland?"

The stiff tone seemed to contradict his polite request, and she couldn't put her finger on what was going on as she slipped out of her coat. When she held it out for him to take, he pinned her with a scowl that was colder than the air outside.

"You're pregnant."

"Yes, I am." Glancing at his wife, she got no help whatsoever, so she focused back on him. "Is that a problem?"

"You didn't mention that when we spoke," he reminded her in an accusing tone.

"I didn't think to. Does it matter?"

"Will your husband be joining you?"

"I'm not married," she answered, bewildered by the sudden hostility. And again, she asked, "Is that a problem?"

Mr. Farrington's lips pressed into a flat, disapproving line, and he all but spat, "We don't rent to tramps like you."

Lindsay felt Brian step up behind her in the protective gesture she remembered so fondly from her difficult high school years. She could feel the fury pouring off him, and she silently begged him not to do anything that would cause the elderly couple to call the sheriff.

"I guess you've got the right to renege on your deal," Brian began in a tone that made it clear what he thought of that, "but the lady sent you a deposit, trusting that there'd be a room waiting for her. She'll be needing that back."

"Didn't sign nothin'," the man argued half-heartedly, probably because he knew Brian was right.

The two glowered at each other, the older one defensive while the younger one simply stared back as if he couldn't believe what he was hearing. After nearly a minute of that, Brian folded his arms in an obstinate way that announced he wasn't leaving until the man refunded Lindsay's down payment to her.

"Ed, just give her the money," his wife pleaded, obviously anxious to have the whole nasty business over with. "I'm sure we can get by without it for a while longer."

He didn't respond but dug a battered wallet from his back pocket and leafed through the contents. Lindsay was fairly certain that he was selecting the most worn bills to give her, and it was all she could do to keep her mouth shut. The whole incident echoed the snobbish way she'd been treated by some of her holier-than-thou classmates, and it was tough not to lash out at the man who'd mashed one of her buttons.

When he finally had the right amount, he pointedly set it on the hallway table before turning and stalking back the way he'd come. It was as if he didn't want to risk catching anything by handing the cash to her, and Lindsay summoned the tattered remnants of her dignity, fighting to keep her temper in check.

"I really am sorry about this, Miss Holland," Mrs. Farrington said quietly as she opened the door for them. "We're in a bad way, and renting that room to you would've made a big difference to all of us. I wish we could have helped each other."

The woman sounded sincere, and Lindsay put aside her own predicament to show some compassion as she retrieved the money that Ed had left. "I do, too. What will you do now?"

"Find another renter, I suppose. It's not easy in the wintertime because folks are pretty well dug in where they are until spring. When you called about our ad, I thought it was the answer to my prayers."

Understandably distraught, she waited for them to leave and eased the door closed behind them. The sound of three different locks engaging ended the uncomfortable confrontation with a finality that sent Lindsay's heart plunging to the snow-covered walkway beneath her feet. Thoroughly soaked from tramping around in her thin flat shoes, they were taking on a decided chill that only made her more miserable. As they headed back to Brian's truck, she felt her heart sinking a little lower with each step.

"Now what?" she asked, glancing back at the house that had seemed so welcoming but had proven to be the exact opposite.

"Lunch. I'm starving."

Her hero, she thought with a fondness that startled her. Over the years, she'd often thought of the rakish boy who'd fought so many battles for her, even before they'd become serious about each other. While he'd been—and still was—one of the best-looking guys she'd ever met, his unswerving willingness to defend her had been the quality she'd admired most about him.

"Okay, but it's on me," she replied, waving the fistful of cash she now held, thanks to him.

"Not a chance. I'm a Calhoun, and we never let a lady pay."

"But—"

"Save your money," he interrupted her as he tossed her bag into the well behind the seat and helped her up into the cab. "You've got a baby on the way, so you're gonna need it."

Baby on the way and no place to live, she added mentally. Technically, she was in the same predicament as yesterday, although the details had changed slightly. The weather hadn't, though, and she shivered despite the warmth of the cab.

"What'm I gonna do?" Hearing the whine in her voice, she cringed and closed her eyes before resting her head on the foggy window.

Brian shifted in his seat, a sure sign that she was making him uncomfortable. Considering how she'd treated him in the past, she felt awful for putting him in the awkward position of being her rescuer. That had been okay when they were younger, but she was a grown woman now, and a mother-to-be besides. No matter how many curve balls life threw at her, she'd have to maneuver her way through them.

Alone.

Forcing herself to look over at him, she gathered up her courage. "I'm sorry, Brian. This is my problem, not yours. I'll figure it out."

Being let off the hook seemed to ease his tension, and he visibly relaxed. "For now, we're gonna get you something to eat. I'm sure Gran has something over at the bakery that'll warm you up."

Ellie Calhoun was one of Lindsay's few fond memories of this place, and just hearing the woman's name made her smile. "That sounds great."

Brian nodded and headed down Main Street toward the tiny business district. She suspected that it had been pretty much the same since the day the founding Calhoun brothers opened their blacksmith shop next to the winding creek that gave the town its name. The stores were small, but each had a large front window that displayed what was sold inside. There was an old-fashioned confectionary, a bookstore that advertised gourmet coffee and a high-speed internet connection, even a small-town barbershop whose striped pole spun in the wind.

Everything was still the way she remembered it, she mused as Brian parked beside Ellie's Bakery and Bike Rentals. That might be a good thing. But considering the way her day had gone so far, she doubted it.

"Lindsay!" When Brian walked her through the glass-front door, his grandmother hurried out from behind the counter to embrace her. Artfully dodging the obvious change in their visitor, she beamed at Lindsay as if she'd been waiting for her all day instead of being surprised to find her there. "It's wonderful to see you. How have you been?"

"Good, and you?"

Gran laughed. "Oh, you know how it is around here. There's always something interesting going on, and I just try to keep up." She turned to Brian with an accusing look. "Why didn't you tell me Lindsay was coming into town?"

"It was a surprise to me, too," he answered, leaning in to kiss her cheek. "I know it's a little early for customers, but what's the chance of us getting some lunch?"

"For my boy? A hundred percent. Since it's so cold, I've got a batch of stew simmering, and I'm just pulling fresh bread out of the oven. You two sit down and I'll bring you some."

"I knew I smelled something amazing," Lindsay commented while she shed her coat.

Suddenly recalling his manners, Brian took it from her and hung it on the rack near the door. Adding his own, he joined her at the table she'd chosen. As far from the front windows as she could get, he noticed. She was either keeping away from the chill near the door or trying to avoid being seen. Considering her condition, he guessed that it was probably some of both.

"I forgot how cold it gets here in the winter," she said, rubbing her bare hands together to warm them. "Once I find myself a job, I'll have to buy a pair of gloves."

"You've got some money now," he reminded her.

"I'll need that to pay for a room. Assuming I can find one."

Brian waited for the cheeky grin he remembered to tell him that she was exaggerating. When it didn't appear, he felt a pang of sorrow for this beautiful, lost woman who'd found herself at the end of her rope and somehow landed on his doorstep. He still wasn't sure how that had happened, but in view of their rocky history he was grateful that despite the obstacles she'd had to overcome, she'd come back to where there were people who genuinely cared about her.

And her baby, he reminded himself, still trying to adjust to the idea. He'd been on his own for years, so he was pretty good at taking care of himself. Someday he'd love to have a family, but right now the idea of assuming responsibility for anyone else scared him to death. Maybe once his business was solidly in the black, he could think about settling down. But these days, struggling to relaunch the ironworks was giving him all he could manage and more.

"How are things going up at your end of town today?" Ellie asked, ruffling his hair.

"Busy. How 'bout here?"

"Oh, you know how it is when the weather's so nasty. Folks just want to tuck in at home and stay warm until the snow stops. They'll be out tomorrow, I'm sure." Her optimism lifted his own spirits, and then she turned her attention to Lindsay. "I'm so proud of this one. He's got so many orders, he won't have time for much else once the forge is up and running."

She hurried back into the kitchen, and Lindsay gave him an accusing look. "I had no idea you had customers waiting for your stuff."

If only the contracts were for more than garden gates and fireplace screens, he thought morosely. But his corporate policy was to be positive around the family to avoid worrying them, so he shrugged. "Yeah, well, I hate to brag."

For the first time since she'd arrived, Lindsay let out an honest laugh. "Since when?"

Since he'd lost three jobs in two years through no fault of his own. He was a skilled machinist, but the shops he'd worked for had been poorly managed, and when they needed to balance the books, he was always the new guy. It had been tough on his ego, and last summer he'd finally had enough of it. Reopening a nineteenth-century business might seem far-fetched to most people, but the effort to resurrect the historic Liberty Creek Forge hadn't just given him something to do. It had gone a long way toward restoring his battered pride.

Because teasing him had brightened her mood, he opted not to share his sob story and instead dredged up a grin. "Good point."

After staring at each other for what felt like a little too long, they fell into an uneasy silence. Then she said, "I see Ellie's still in town. How about the rest of your family?"

"Sam got married just before Christmas," he replied, grateful for something else to talk about. "He and Holly live on the edge of town with her son, Chase, who's just about the greatest kid ever. Emma teaches art at the elementary school and lives in our old house. Mom and Dad both work over in Waterford now, so they moved there a few years ago."

"Have you been here all this time?"

"I moved around a bit, then settled in Portsmouth for a while before coming back. I wasn't sure about it at first, but it's really nice to be home."

"That doesn't surprise me," she commented as Gran approached their table carrying a loaded tray. "You never struck me as the nomad type."

Unlike her, Brian added silently. He wondered if that would change now that she had a child to consider.

"Here you go, kids," Gran announced, setting their lunch out for them.

He'd skipped breakfast that morning, and the aroma of her blue-ribbon cooking actually made his mouth water. He tore off a piece of bread and dipped it into the steaming crock of stew before popping it in his mouth. Registering his grandmother's questioning look, he chuckled. "You've been experimenting again, haven't you?"

"Maybe. Can you tell what's different?"

"Delicious as usual," he replied because quite honestly, he couldn't detect anything beyond that.

She gave him a chiding look before turning to Lindsay, who smiled. "There's a hint of cayenne pepper in here, right?"

Gran pressed her hands together in delight. "That's right! I've had a dozen people taste this, and you're the first one to guess my secret ingredient."

"I didn't think you liked spicy food," Brian said, more than a little confused. Apparently, her pregnancy wasn't the only thing about Lindsay Holland that was different. It made him wonder what else someone might discover if he tried hard enough to peel back some of those self-protective layers she'd wrapped herself in. Of course, it wouldn't be him, he amended quickly. She'd burned him once, and he wasn't about to step into range and give her the chance to do it again.

"The baby does," she confided with a little grin. "Whenever I eat something hot, she does backflips."

"It's a girl?" Gran asked.

"I'm hoping so. I'd have no idea what to do with a boy."

"You'd figure it out, just like the rest of us. Having a child is wonderful, no matter who we're mothering."

"Thank you for saying that. I think it's wonderful, too, although I have to be honest. Not many people agree with me."

Gran waved that off as if it was no concern at all. "That's their problem. Children are a blessing straight from heaven itself, and you've got every reason to be happy about this one. There's a new couple at our church who's been trying for years to have a baby but can't. They've started the adoption process because they want a family so much, but they're finding out that it takes a long time to be approved."

Something sparked in Lindsay's eyes, and while she didn't comment, Brian could see the wheels spinning in that quick mind that had always amazed him. Whatever it was, it passed as quickly as it had appeared. He still felt uneasy, because he had no clue what was going on with her.

That thought led to another, more pressing one. "Gran, Lindsay's looking for a place to stay. Do you know of anyone who's got a room to rent here in town?"

After thinking for a few moments, she shook her head. "But I've got a big house with plenty of guest rooms, Lindsay. You're welcome to stay with me until you find something more permanent."

"I don't want to impose on you," Lindsay protested.

"Please," Gran scoffed. "The house echoes like the Grand Canyon, it's so quiet. I'd love to have some company, even if it's only for a little while."

"Well, okay," Lindsay finally agreed, adding a grateful smile that would have softened a heart made of granite. "Thank you."

They finished the rest of their lunch in near silence, and Brian figured it was because they really had nothing left to say. More than once over the years, he'd wondered how it would be to see his blue-eyed gypsy again. Needless to say, this really wasn't the way he'd pictured it.

She was finally warm.

After a long, difficult day, Lindsay woke up tucked into one of Ellie's comfy guest rooms, snuggled in blissfully soft sheets beneath a pile of what were surely handmade quilts. She had an entire queen-size bed to herself, and more fluffy pillows than she knew what to do with.

It was dark outside the window, and she checked the old-fashioned alarm clock to find it was almost seven o'clock. And she was starving. Her lunch with Brian had tasted like cayenne-flavored sawdust, so she'd eaten only enough to satisfy his insistence that she should have something to eat. Turning on the bedside lamp, she found her shoes in the closet and stepped into them, only to discover that they were still soaking wet. Beside them was a worn pair of fleece-lined slippers that looked to be about her size, so she pulled them on instead. Padding across the richly colored wood floor, she eased the door open and strained her ears for a hint of the conversation going on below.

"What do you want me to do, Gran?" Brian's unmistakable baritone demanded in a hushed tone. "This is my business we're talking about. I've put everything I've got into it, and then some. I've only got one shot at making this work, and I can't hire someone I don't have complete faith in."

"You need an office manager," Ellie argued in the sensible New Englander way Lindsay recalled from her childhood, "and Lindsay just happens to be an experienced one who's looking for a job. Do you think she's capable of doing what you need done?"

After a long pause, he grudgingly admitted, "Probably."

"If you're not sure about that, you should call her last boss and ask what he thought of her. Then you can feel more confident about your choice, whatever you decide."

"I feel sorry for Lindsay, but I'm not hiring her, end of story." The sound of chair legs scraping across the kitchen floor reached upstairs, and she heard something in his voice she hadn't expected: regret. "That storm's getting worse, and the snow is piling up out there. I'll be back in the morning to shovel the driveway and front walk for you before you go into the bakery at eight."

"Thank you, honey. I appreciate you taking care of it. Don't work too late tonight."

"I won't."

The door opened and then closed, and then all was quiet.

Lindsay's appetite had evaporated during the terse conversation she'd overheard, and she crept back to bed. Despite his earlier refusal to hire her, she'd sensed that he wasn't completely convinced about it. That had left her with a tiny sliver of hope that he might change his mind, especially when she heard Ellie gently nudging him to reconsider. His comment about not being able to trust her made her more ashamed than she'd ever been, and she buried herself under the covers while tears that she'd held in for days finally escaped.

Working for Brian had been her last—and only—chance at some security for herself and her unborn child. Now that door was firmly closed, and she searched her mind for the window that the old saying insisted would be opened.

But this time, there wasn't one.

Chapter Three

After a few hours of restless sleep, Brian finally gave up and decided it was time to start his day. The caretaker's cottage next to the forge was pretty bare-bones, even for him, and he wasn't surprised when he poked his head out from under the covers only to discover there was no heat. Again.

He was good with most machinery, but the antique oil furnace bewildered him. No matter what fix he tried, it refused to fire up without some serious coaxing. Fortunately, the small fieldstone fireplace was more reliable. Too bad he'd forgotten to bank the fire before hitting the hay last night.

Rather than waste time building another one, he settled for a steamy shower that not only warmed him up but also eased some of the lingering pain from yesterday. Every muscle in his body ached from wrestling with the archaic equipment he was trying to bring back from the dead, and he faced another long day of the same. His daunting rehab project had been going on for six months now, and sometimes he wondered if he was making any progress at all.

Pushing the doubt from his mind, he strolled into the lobby and silently thanked whoever had invented a coffee maker that could fill up his mug in less than a minute. Wrapping his cold hands around the warm ceramic, he snagged a power bar and opened one of the huge doors to the old-fashioned blacksmith shop that was the heart and soul of his family's once-thriving business. Repairs to the building itself had taken forever, from the roof to evicting a family of chipmunks that had taken up residence in the flue of the enormous fireplace that had literally forged the existence of Liberty Creek and other small towns for miles around.

Since its opening, everything from wagon wheels to bucket hoops to cast-iron pots were produced here by Jeremiah Calhoun and his brothers, one piece at a time. Now that he was picking up the torch, Brian felt a kinship with them that gave him a tremendous sense of pride. He'd enjoyed the variety of living in other places, and when he first mentioned leaving the bustle of Portsmouth and returning to his sleepy hometown, most of his friends were convinced he'd gone and lost his mind. But as difficult as things could be for him at times, he never doubted that he'd made the right decision.

Well, almost never.

When his cell phone's old-time telephone ringer sounded, he glanced at the screen to discover that the environmental inspector who'd been assigned to his project was calling. It was just after seven, and he suspected that the man wasn't contacting him to share good news. Brian recalled hearing once that a smile could be heard over the phone, so he forced one onto his face before answering. "Hello, Mr. Williams. What can I do for you?"

"I've found a conflict with the appointment we made for the final inspection of your air scrubbing system at the end of the month. I apologize for the short notice, but there's no way around it. I have an opening at nine on Thursday morning if you can do it then."

Brian had installed the equipment, but the complicated job had gobbled up all of his time for more than a week. That meant the mound of paperwork that he was supposed to fill out was still sitting on his desk, blank as the day the inspector had handed it to him. "That's the day after tomorrow, so I'm not sure. Is there another option?"

"May."

"Really?" Brian blurted without thinking. "That's a long time to wait."

"There aren't many people in the country who do what I do, so my calendar is booked solid until then. Should we schedule something in May?"

The tourists that were the lifeblood of the local economy typically started visiting in late spring, and if something went wrong with an inspection in May, Brian wouldn't be able to fix it in time to welcome customers to his shop. That would jeopardize not only his current plans, but might also dissuade Jordan from leaving his successful artisan career and joining the company. If that happened, Brian couldn't possibly hope to meet the high expectations of the discerning clients he wanted to reach. Without the benefit of Jordan's contacts and expertise, Brian knew that he might as well save himself the aggravation and close the doors now.

"Thursday's fine," he gritted out, hoping his irritation wasn't too obvious. "I'll see you then."

He hung up, then closed his eyes and held the phone

against his forehead. There were days when he wondered if the crazy scheme he'd concocted was worth the overwhelming effort he was putting into it. This was one of them, and to make it worse, setbacks like this made him doubt whether it was even possible for him to bring the long-dormant shop back to life.

Lifting his head, he took in his outdated surroundings in a more critical fashion than he had so far. The tools of his trade hadn't changed all that much over the centuries—fire and force were still the essential components of metalworking. Above the fireplace, currently out of sight, was the problematic—and very expensive—air scrubber that was the key to him being certified to operate his coal-fired forge the old-fashioned way.

Aside from that, the vast collection of hammers, snips and anvils of various shapes were all he needed to fill his customers' orders. But none of that mattered if he didn't pass Mr. Williams's inspection in two days, he reminded himself grimly. A rebel at heart, following other people's rules had never been his strong point, and recalling the intimidating stack of forms made him want to scream in frustration.

Doing something physical was usually the cure for that, and he'd promised to dig Gran out this morning, anyway. His four-by-four crawled out of its spot without a problem, and he made the quick trip across town through a gray, frigid dawn that didn't feel very promising. When he arrived at her house, he grabbed a shovel from its spot in the old carriage house and got to work.

One shovelful at a time. In his memory, he heard Granddad's voice telling him that when he was a little boy doing his best to help with the wintertime task. *That's how even the biggest job gets done.*

Stunned by the clarity of the message and how well suited it was to his current problem, Brian stopped and rested his gloves on the handle of the shovel. Listening closely, he didn't pick up anything other than the rumble of a nearby plow and the rustling of bare tree branches in the breeze.

Had it been his imagination? he wondered. Tired as he was, it was a definite possibility that his mind was playing tricks on him, conjuring up some reassuring words from his grandfather to help him through a crisis.

"Is everything okay?"

Startled by the sound of an actual voice, Brian whipped around to find Lindsay standing inside the open front door, head tilted while she stared at him in obvious concern. In her hands she held an oversize coffee mug, steaming in the chilly air.

"Yeah, just taking a breather. What're you doing up so early?"

"I couldn't sleep anymore, so I'm making breakfast for Ellie. When I heard you out here, I thought you might like something warm to drink."

It was a thoughtful thing to do, especially considering that just a few hours ago, he'd flatly refused to hire her. The faint pang of guilt he'd been feeling grew stronger, and he began to second-guess his decision. "Thanks for thinking of it. You shouldn't be out here, though. It's freezing."

That got him a wry grin. "I'm tougher than I look."

Yeah, she was, he remembered with more fondness than he would have preferred. Her delicate appearance masked a headstrong temperament that had proven to be more than a handful in their younger days. It was good to know that her current predicament hadn't completely shattered the spirit he'd once admired so much.

"I'll come in and thaw out," he said, climbing the snowy steps to join her. "I'm ready for a break, anyway."

After shedding his ice-caked boots and coat in the entryway, he followed Lindsay into the warm, welcoming space that was his grandmother's little kingdom. Gifted with culinary talent and a knack for inventing new dishes, Gran had fed hundreds of family and friends over the years from the bright, unassuming kitchen that was her domain.

Lindsay opened the warming drawer of the commercial oven, and the scent of fresh pancakes made Brian's empty stomach growl. She laughed, pulling several out to set on a plate for him. "It sounds like you're hungry."

"Starving. Thanks."

He slathered on butter and drowned them in syrup that had come from maple trees outside of town. He was demolishing them when his grandmother came down the creaky wooden steps and into the kitchen.

"Good morning," she greeted him, pausing to kiss the top of his head as if he was ten years old.

"Mmmng," he mumbled around a mouthful of pancakes.

She laughed and crossed the floor to pour hot water from the teakettle into a flowered china cup. "He sounds happy. How are you feeling this morning, Lindsay?"

"Fine, thanks."

Brian quickly swallowed and asked, "Feeling? Were you sick yesterday?"

"Tired more than anything, I think. It comes with the territory," she added, smoothing her hands over her plump waistline. "Growing a person is hard work."

Brian had all he could do growing his business, and he couldn't begin to imagine how difficult her task was. Thinking of the forge reminded him of the impending deadline he now faced, and he realized that the solution to his problem was standing in his grandmother's kitchen, spooning batter onto the griddle.

"Lindsay?" When she turned to glance at him, he swallowed his pride with some coffee and prepared his stomach for a bitter helping of crow. "I've got a major problem at the ironworks." He explained it to her, ending with, "I'm still finishing up the installation of the unit, and there's no way I can get everything done on my own. Would you consider taking that office manager job, after all?"

"Yes."

Her answer came without hesitation, and he could hardly believe it. He'd anticipated her yanking his chain a little, perhaps making him grovel for entertainment's sake. She didn't even ask him how long their arrangement would last. It told him just how desperate she was, and he felt awful for the way he'd handled things with her yesterday. He didn't want them starting off with any illusions about the position, so he cautioned her, "I'm not sure how much work I'll have for you after that."

"That's okay," she responded brightly. "Once you see what I can do, you might decide you can't get along without me."

"And you're welcome to stay here as long as you want," Gran assured her with a smile. "I really enjoy having the company, and I can drop you off at the ironworks when I drive into the bakery."

"That's sweet of you, and I'd be happy to take you up on it. As a tenant."

"Oh, posh," Gran scoffed, waving away the offer. "That's not necessary."

"It is for me," Lindsay insisted, sitting in the chair beside his grandmother. "I'm going to be a mom soon, and I need to be more responsible than I have been in the past. That means not letting people do things for me that I can do for myself."

Gran sent him a questioning look, and he shrugged slightly. It was up to her, really, but he had to admit he was impressed by Lindsay's insistence on paying her own way. Prompted by Jeff's behavior, no doubt. In Brian's opinion, it was definitely a change for the better.

The skunk may have actually done her a favor, he mused while he mopped up his syrup with the last of his pancakes. Maybe she'd needed to hit rock bottom to realize just how bad things had gotten.

Now there was no place for her to go but up. And if anyone he knew had the will to make that happen, it was Lindsay Holland.

Lindsay was in the middle of the daunting stack of paperwork when a tiny elbow poked her hard enough to snag her immediate attention. Massaging the spot, she kept moving in a circular motion until the little troublemaker inside her rolled over into a different position that was more comfortable.

For a few minutes, anyway.

She'd been feeling the baby move for weeks now, but sometimes she still marveled at those simple reminders that there was a small person growing inside of her. The jabs came at all times of the day, so they were always a surprise to her, making her wonder if the restlessness was a hint at the personality to come. And if it was, how would she cope with raising such an active child all by herself?

Her own mother hadn't managed the task all that well, and while Lindsay recognized that she'd been a handful, she'd often felt that Mom could have tried harder to bond with her independent-minded daughter. After all, Lindsay had come by her stubbornness innocently enough, inheriting not only her mother's looks but her headstrong attitude, as well.

It seemed disloyal to feel that way, and as she'd matured, Lindsay had come to understand that Mom had done the best she could. Too bad it hadn't even come close to what an insecure teenage girl needed.

The baby was now resting calmly under her hand, and she smiled down to where her palm rested. "I promise to always be there for you, little one, no matter what."

She sensed a flutter of movement, as if her child had heard the vow and was acknowledging it. It was times like these when she—as nonreligious as a person could get—honestly believed in miracles.

A motion in the doorway caught her attention, and she glanced up to find Brian leaning against the jamb, arms crossed while he gazed curiously at her. "How's it going in here?"

"Good," she replied, patting the growing pile of finished paperwork proudly. "I just went past halfway."

"So it's downhill from here, then?"

In her experience, that wasn't how things worked. But Brian was up against a nearly impossible deadline, and she decided that there wasn't any point in being negative about their chances of actually finishing in time. "Like a snowball picking up speed."

Cocking his head, he grinned at her. "You don't really believe that, do you?"

Stunned that he'd seen through her attempt at levity, she blinked. Either he read her better than most people did, or she was losing her ability to smooth over difficult situations with a little well-placed deceit. Whichever was accurate, it didn't bode well for her continuing to work with someone who'd hired her out of desperation and had no reason to keep her on once this crisis had passed.

"Don't look so panicky," he said in a reassuring tone as he came into the office. "I'm not judging you or anything. Since we're gonna be working together, I was thinking it might go better if we're straight with each other."

Relief washed over her, and she forced a shaky smile. "Oh. Okay."

Spinning a rickety-looking folding chair around, he crossed his arms on the back and sat facing her. "So, whatta you really think?"

"It will be tight, but I'll get it done." Bravado aside, she got the feeling that it was time to finally put their difficult history in the rearview. For both of them. "I know I haven't always been trustworthy in the past, Brian, but I'm working really hard to change that."

"Because of the baby?"

"Mostly."

"What about for yourself?" She wasn't sure how to respond to that, and after a few moments, he continued, "You deserve better than you've gotten, Lindsay. You're smart and funny, and you've got a good heart. Have you ever thought about what you wanted, just for you?"

"College would've been nice," she admitted shyly,

hesitant to voice a wish that had proven to be too far
out of reach for her. "I always wanted to— Never mind.
It's too crazy."

That made him laugh, and she saw the humor lighting his eyes in the way she remembered so fondly.

"Look around," he said, holding his arms out in em-
phasis. "I'm restoring a business to run the way it did
in the 1800s. Anything you come up with won't be half
as crazy as what I'm doing here."

His confidence and reassuring words eased her hesitance, and she decided to go for it. At the worst, he'd
laugh. At the best, he'd understand how it felt to have
a dream that everyone else thought was unattainable.
"I've always wanted to be a family therapist. You know,
counsel kids and their families who are having a tough
time, help them learn a better way to handle things."

"You've got some experience with that," he said gently,
sympathy warming the blue in his eyes to something
she could almost feel from across the desk.

"Yeah, and I've often wondered if Mom and I would've
done better if someone had taught us a better way of dealing with each other."

"Life gets harder all the time, it seems," he commented in a pensive tone. "My childhood here was awesome, but the older I get, the faster the world seems to
spin. I can't imagine how tough it is for kids these days."

"It's hard for grown-ups, too," Lindsay added, hearing enthusiasm in her voice for the first time in what
felt like forever. "Struggling families aren't good for
anyone, but especially for the kids involved. I really
believe that a little help at the right time can make all
the difference."

"So why didn't you pursue that? You were always

a great student, and you were definitely smart enough to do well in college."

"Money, for one."

"There's all kinds of scholarships out there," he argued, as if him saying it was enough to make it happen. And for Brian, someone full of talent and self-confidence, it was probably true.

But for her, the real problem had been something she'd never been able to define. With him sitting there, urging her to seriously consider the dream she'd abandoned so long ago, she finally had to admit the truth. To herself.

"Jeff didn't think I should do it," she said in a meek, doormat voice that made her want to cringe. "He said we couldn't afford to lose my salary and waste money on something that might not pan out. After a while, I guess I started to believe him."

Brian's jaw clenched around something he was clearly dying to say but wouldn't because he respected her feelings. She couldn't recall the last time anyone had kept an opinion to themselves out of concern for how it might hurt her.

It was comforting to know that—unlike so many people who'd run through her chaotic life—Brian Calhoun hadn't changed. He still cared about her, and even though she'd blown her one chance with him, he'd make a great friend, she realized. A girl in her situation could never have too many of those.

"He was wrong," Brian finally spat, his words heavily salted with disdain. "You can do whatever you set your mind to, Lindsay. Now that you're away from him, I hope you'll forget everything he ever told you and be able to focus on what's best for you and the baby. Anything else is just noise, as far as I can see."

"Focus," she echoed, tilting her head while she considered his advice. "You're right. That's exactly what I need. What I always needed," she admitted, shaking her head as things crystallized in her mind. "I just never found a way to get it."

"You were too distracted, trying to get past your mom's reputation and make people like you. Then you met Jeff, and you lost sight of everything else."

Lost was exactly how she'd felt her entire life, she realized with a clarity so sudden it felt like a starburst in her mind. Except for when a small-town boy had reached out and offered her not only his attention but his love.

And how did she repay his generosity? She turned away from everything he represented, leaping into an uncertain future with a man who'd later stolen her ability to provide for the innocent child he'd abandoned when he left her.

When her morose thoughts receded, she realized that Brian had stood and was leaving the office.

"Brian?" When he glanced back, she swallowed hard and forced herself to do something she now knew she should have done years ago. "I'm sorry I hurt you. I never meant to."

A brief flash of affection lit his eyes, and he gave her the crooked grin that brought to mind the way he'd looked the very first time she met him. "I know."

With that, he left her and returned to the baffling array of equipment waiting for him out in the shop. As he went, she could faintly hear him whistling the same song he'd been listening to when she showed up at the forge yesterday. He knew it was her favorite, so she didn't doubt that he was making the musical gesture very much on purpose.

And for the first time in ages, Lindsay allowed herself to believe that after years of wrong turns and bad decisions, things might finally be okay.

Chapter Four

"That's what you're wearing?" Lindsay demanded when she met Brian in the office the morning of their all-important inspection.

"You've been working for me less than a week," he reminded her with a grin. "If you wanna critique my wardrobe, you've gotta stick it out for a whole year."

He did notice, however, that she was wearing a pretty maternity dress that tied in the back and polished black shoes instead of the tired ones she'd had on yesterday. She'd confessed that she didn't have much in the way of mom-to-be clothing, and he'd already seen the extent of it. Or so he thought.

"That's pretty," he complimented her as she handed him a mug of what smelled like hazelnut coffee. "Is it new?"

"To me it is." She gave him a long, suspicious look. "Someone told your sister-in-law, Holly, that I needed maternity clothes, and she dropped off four bags of them at Ellie's house last night."

"I didn't say anything, so don't look at me like that. Must've been Gran."

"Well, whoever it was, I appreciate it," she commented, smiling as she ran a hand over a long sleeve. "This is a lot warmer than anything I had before, and Holly has excellent taste. I haven't had anything this nice in years."

The wistful tone did something wonky to his stomach, and Brian caught himself wishing there was something he could do to erase those bad times from her memory. Then he heard his father's wise advice.

If you're not the problem, you can't be the solution.

Simple but true, those words echoed in his mind even as he worked his way back to what had started the conversation. "Speaking of nice, what's wrong with what I'm wearing?"

"You're meeting with the environmental inspector today, remember?"

"No, that's on Thursday."

Lindsay gave him a quizzical look, then shook her head with an irritating smirk. "Today is Thursday."

"Seriously?" When she nodded, he checked his wrist, which was empty because he'd never worn a watch in his life. "Huh. How 'bout that? Guess it's a good thing I hired you to keep me up to date on stuff like that."

"I'd say so," she agreed. "Now, march back over and put on your Sunday best. He's due here at nine."

"It's only eight."

"You need to crank up the heat in the shop and fire up the forge to show him that the air scrubbers are working properly. While you're doing that, I'll make a carafe of coffee and set these out," she added, patting the top of a pink bakery box imprinted with Ellie's Bakery and Bike Rentals in burgundy script. "He's already on the road, and I wouldn't be surprised if he's hungry when he gets here."

"Man, you think of everything," he said as he headed for the door.

"Isn't that why you hired me?"

Pausing, he turned and noticed the hesitant look on her face. After all she'd been through, it wasn't a surprise to him that her confidence had taken a knock. Sure, she'd left him hanging and basically run away rather than work things out with him. It had taken him a while to get over her, but in the end, he'd accepted that things had turned out the way they were meant to be.

Until the morning she showed up at the forge, out of options and hoping for a job. He hadn't recognized it until now, but that day had changed everything. For both of them.

He wasn't interested in a relationship right now, especially not with someone toting around as much baggage as Lindsay Holland. Fortunately, his own personal baggage was pretty light these days. Based on their experience so far, he thought it was possible that he could be the friend she so clearly needed. "It sure is. Now that you mention cold, it's not exactly warm in here, either. Did that space heater conk out on you?"

"No, I like it this way," she replied in a thoughtful tone as her eyes drifted toward the mullioned window that looked out on the side yard covered in snow. "I love winter."

He remembered that about her. How she adored iceskating and was always game for a snowball fight or an afternoon at the community sledding hill just outside of town. The first real snowfall was her favorite, and he recalled her insisting that those snowflakes were the most delicious ones of the season because they were fresh.

"Brian?"

Dragged back to grown-up reality, he met her stare with what he hoped came across as casual interest. "Yeah?"

In answer, she tapped the antique watch on her wrist. Brian recognized it immediately, and an emotion he didn't recognize flooded his chest. "You still have that?"

"Of course, I do," she replied with a shadow of the beautiful smile he still remembered. "The antique show we went to on my birthday that year was one of the best afternoons of my whole life. No one had ever gone to so much trouble to make sure I had a good time. That you bought me such a gorgeous present was just icing on the cake."

"I just thought that since you were so strapped for cash, you would've sold it by now."

"Not a chance," she assured him, tilting her chin in a defiant gesture that hinted at the spirit that had once enchanted and aggravated him. "I sold off everything I had, which wasn't much, but I'd never give this up. It's really special, because you gave it to me without expecting anything from me in return."

Knowing that the watch he'd given her was the only jewelry she still owned emphasized the sobering fact that if he failed this environmental inspection and his business faltered, this vulnerable woman and her child would be in major trouble. Prodded into action, he hurried back to his house to change.

He really had to get a grip where Lindsay was concerned, he warned himself while he shrugged on his nicest shirt and quickly did the buttons. If he wasn't careful, the blue-eyed gypsy who'd broken his heart all those years ago was going to get under his skin and cause him all kinds of problems.

Again.

Shrugging away the past, he went through the side door of the forge and cranked the old heating furnace to full power. Then he snapped on all the lights and scaled the narrow metal steps that led to the catwalk running along the west end of the shop to ensure that everything was in place. The crucial piece of equipment that would—hopefully—allow him to operate his dinosaur of a forge in the modern world was as he'd left it early this morning. From its size and basic-looking construction, you'd never have guessed that the metal box and the pipes leading to it were going to make or break the future of his business.

Pass the inspection, it was full-steam ahead. Fail…

He wasn't going to think about that, he decided firmly, batting the very real possibility aside. He was taking his shot at the moon, and fly or crash, he knew he'd done everything in his power to make it work. Well, almost.

Glancing up, he cocked his head and quietly said, "I know You're real busy, but if You've got time, a little help would be great."

Of course, he wouldn't know if his prayer had been heard until Mr. Williams gave him the results of his assessment, Brian reminded himself as he carefully descended to the shop floor. That was the thing about the Almighty. Sometimes you had to wait for an answer, and even then you might not get the one you wanted. Then you had to take what He gave you and make the best of it.

That was why they called it faith.

Oddly enough, that thought boosted his spirits, and despite getting only a few hours of sleep, he felt pretty chipper as he headed into the lobby.

Lindsay met him in the seating area, which she'd given a very practical makeover so it was much more presentable to guests. Giving him a quick once-over that ended in a smile, she murmured, "Much better. Now you look like a bona fide businessman."

"Thanks. Speaking of business, I was thinking…" He paused, giving the idea one more careful thought before deciding to charge ahead. "Once we get through this, make a list of what you think this place needs to get started out on the right foot."

Truthfully, he couldn't afford much, and he even doubted that he could manage to pay her for more than a few months. But Lindsay was stranded with nowhere else to go, and he simply couldn't stand by and watch her suffer through the rest of her pregnancy alone.

"Does that mean you'll hire me permanently?" she asked hopefully.

His chest constricted. Maybe if she knew about the shoestring budget he was confined to, she'd leave and save him the trouble of inventing a logical reason not to bring her on.

"Well, as you can see from the office and in here—" he spread his hands to indicate the mostly empty reception area "—I'm starting from scratch. I need someone who can do a lot with not very much and come up with ways to help me make this place tread water until Jordan gets here in the fall."

"Do you have a website?"

Two steps ahead of him, as usual. But there was no

way he was telling her that, so he shook his head. "I'm not a computer guy. Remember?"

"Well, that's the place to start. Boutique companies like this need an online presence and storefront. That allows you to sell products to customers who've never even heard of Liberty Creek. Plus, you can track costs, inventory, payroll, taxes—all the important things that every business owner needs to have a handle on."

The way she rattled off the list impressed him, and he grinned. "You sound like you know what you're talking about."

"After I worked for that law firm I mentioned, I was a temp for an agency that supplied legal admin help. I learned a lot, bouncing from one office to another."

Brian heard the hesitance creeping back into her tone, and he debated whether or not to pursue the subject any further. She wasn't his responsibility, but his gut was leaning toward hiring her. After some more mental tug-of-war, he swallowed his misgivings and leaped. "I can't pay you much, and it's part-time, but we can give it a shot."

Joy drove the anxiety from her eyes, and she stood on tiptoe to hug him. As if realizing what she'd done, she quickly pulled back and beamed up at him. "Thank you, Brian. I know we didn't end up at a good place before, but I promise not to let you down this time."

Given their history, he wasn't sure about that, but he forced a smile to avoid upsetting her. What's the worst that could happen? They decided they couldn't work together and ended up going their separate ways. He'd lived through that with her once and it hadn't killed him. Chances were he could do it again.

"So," she went on in a gentle tone. "Are you nervous about today?"

Relieved to have it in the open, he blew out a steadying breath. "You have no idea."

"I don't know about the mechanical stuff, but your paperwork's done. I copied it at the bakery this morning. Ellie was more than happy to let me use her copier."

"Aw, man." He sighed. "I never would've thought of doing that."

"That's not your job. It's mine."

Their last-minute arrangement seemed to be working, with him doing the hands-on stuff and her handling the administrative end of things. He was still leery of leaning too heavily on her, but he had to admit that so far, they made a pretty good team.

Fortunately for his jangling nerves, the inspector was the punctual type, and a gray sedan was just pulling into the parking area. The suspense would be over soon, Brian mused wryly. One way or another.

When the door opened, he put on his friendliest face and walked over to meet his guest. Reminding himself to keep it simple, he held out his hand. "Good morning, Mr. Williams. I'm Brian Calhoun, and this is my office manager, Lindsay Holland. Welcome to Liberty Creek Forge."

The middle-aged man wore a navy suit and rimless glasses that were fogging over in the warmer air inside the building. After shaking Brian's hand, he wiped them on his scarf and gave the area a brief look before strolling through the hallway, stopping outside the open shop doors. Interest lit his dark eyes, and he turned to Brian. "You said this was a legacy blacksmith shop, but I didn't realize everything was original to the building."

Brian wasn't sure how to take that, but he opted for a positive approach. "The tools haven't changed much over the years, so if they're not broken, we don't replace them."

"This is your family's business, then?"

"Since 1820," Brian informed him proudly.

"Fascinating."

"May I take your coat, Mr. Williams?" Lindsay asked with one of her more dazzling smiles.

Clearly flattered by the attention, he returned the gesture as he shrugged off his wool dress coat. "Thank you, Ms. Holland."

"Oh, please," she batted away the formality with her free hand. "Call me Lindsay. It's cold out there, so I picked up some Danish and made fresh coffee. Would you like any of either before you get started?"

"Both would be wonderful, thank you."

"You're very welcome."

Walking ahead of him in the swaying motion Brian was still getting accustomed to, she was chattering away, giving him details about the history of the forge that sounded as if they were straight out of a local history book. By the time the three of them reached the office, Brian was beginning to think that Lindsay could have managed the entire interview all by herself.

Almost before he was sitting at the worktable she'd set up for him, Lindsay made sure their visitor had a mug imprinted with the forge's logo and one of Gran's melt-in-your-mouth cheese Danish. Then, blinding him with another warm smile, she pointed toward the desk and said, "I'll leave the hard work to you two. I'll be right over here if you need anything."

The inspector thanked her again, and gave Brian

an impressed look. "I thought this was going to be one of those struggling small-town companies I so often visit. Hiring competent staff is the mark of a smart businessman."

"Yeah, she's something else." Brian caught her smirk out of the corner of his eye and added, "Would you excuse us a minute? We have a few things to go over for today."

"Take your time," their guest agreed, flipping open a small laptop that quickly hummed to life. "I'll look through the information you've compiled and make notes of anything that requires more attention."

Great, Brian groused silently, anticipating that the list would be long and painful. Since he hadn't actually read any of the requirements for himself, he had no clue whether or not Lindsay had been able to pull all the documentation together. But there was no help for that now, so he settled for motioning her out front where they could speak in private.

"Flirting with the inspector, Holland?" he demanded in a whisper. "What're you thinking?"

"That he's a man, and many of the men I've met like a little ego boost whenever they can get one."

"Is that really a good idea in this situation? You came on pretty strong in there."

His outrage earned him a full-circle roll of those gorgeous baby blues. "He's married, you idiot. I wouldn't have done it otherwise."

Brian hadn't noticed a wedding ring, but then again he wasn't in the habit of checking out things like that. Knowing that she was didn't exactly sit right with him, but there didn't seem to be any harm done, so he opted to let it go. "Fine, but from now on, take it easy on our visitors. We don't wanna have to call the paramedics because you turned the charm on a little too hard."

She gave him a curious look, then a little smile lifted her mouth into the very tempting bow shape his younger self had always had a hard time resisting. "You really think I have that much charm? Even now?" she pressed, holding her arms out wide.

He honestly did, but if he told her so, he suspected that she'd never let him live it down. "I'm just saying you should be more careful how you behave around men you don't know. That's all."

The playfulness left her features, and she studied him intently. "You're absolutely right, and I apologize if I went overboard. I realize that I'm representing Liberty Creek Forge to the outside world, and I promise to be more professional in the future."

That wasn't really what he'd meant, and it startled him to realize that he'd been more concerned for her personally than about how her behavior could impact his business. "Thanks. I'd appreciate it."

"Anytime, boss."

Flashing him a bright—but not flirtatious—grin, she went back into the office and sat primly behind the desk to continue going through a box filled with old files that probably hadn't seen the light of day since before Brian was born. Busywork, she'd called it, to make her appear occupied but interruptable in case the inspector needed her to clarify something for him.

Brian had never worked in an office, so he had no clue what she was talking about. Normally, his days began when he woke up and ended when he finally fell into bed, too exhausted to notice how cold his unheated bedroom was. But today he had to at least act like the owner of a potentially successful blacksmith shop. After a long look into the production space where he felt so at home, he reluctantly dragged his feet back toward where his very official guest was waiting for him.

Praying that, somehow, this time tomorrow he'd still be in business.

"Surprise!"

Lindsay nearly jumped out of her skin when Ellie's darkened living room lit up in a burst of lights and more than a dozen Calhouns appeared from their hiding places. Brian stepped in front of her in a protective motion that quickly eased her fright into something more palatable. Apparently, he'd been just as shocked as she had, and he retreated with a laugh. "You guys scared the life outta me."

"Congratulations, honey," his mother, Melinda, sang, coming forward to embrace him proudly. "We all knew you'd get through that inspection with flying colors."

"Yeah?" he teased, eyebrow cocked in amusement. "Then why all the hoopla? You could've just called to congratulate me."

"Nonsense," she scoffed, smacking his shoulder as Steve joined her, grinning with pride for his son's accomplishment. Then, to Lindsay's astonishment, Brian half turned and gently drew her forward. "I couldn't have done it without Lindsay. She's a whiz at cutting through red tape."

"I'm not surprised a bit," Melinda commented, folding Lindsay into a warm hug. "You were always so bright, and your legal expertise must have prepared you for all kinds of tough jobs. It's wonderful to see you again."

To the woman's credit, her eyes stayed fixed on Lindsay's, without even a glance at her widening middle. Lindsay hadn't seen these people in years, and yet they seemed to know all about what she'd been up to. "It's great to see you, too. Brian must've filled you in on—" she paused, uncertain of the correct way to phrase her thought, so she settled on "—everything."

Melinda and a young woman nearby laughed as if they'd just heard the best joke ever.

"Brian?" the other woman echoed in a melodic Southern accent, sending him an aggravated look. "Not hardly. It's great to meet you," she added, offering her hand. "I'm Sam's wife, Holly."

Lindsay couldn't wrap her head around the idea that this beaming, friendly woman was married to Brian's reserved older brother. Then again, maybe he'd changed since she'd last seen him. So many things had. "It's great to meet you, too. Thanks so much for the clothes you left at Ellie's for me. It was really sweet of you."

"You're welcome. I know how expensive maternity stuff is, and I'm glad someone else can get some use out of those outfits. We moms have to stick together, don't we?"

Intellectually, Lindsay understood that she was going to be a mother soon, but she didn't often discuss it with anyone. Especially not a complete stranger. To hear Holly so breezily include her in that category made Lindsay uncomfortable for some reason. To her relief, Holly went on.

"So, Ellie says you've been in Ohio. How do you like being back in Liberty Creek?"

"Much better," Lindsay replied as she slipped out of the coat that hadn't buttoned in weeks.

Brian glanced around and asked, "Where's your mom?"

"On a ship somewhere in the Aegean," Holly replied, shaking her head. "This is her first winter in a long time, and a couple weeks ago, she'd finally had enough. She's visiting friends around Greece and Europe, then meeting up with Oliver and his grandsons in Rome."

"Wow," Lindsay said, stunned by the dizzying itinerary. "She knows people all over the world."

"Daphne Mills never met anyone she couldn't have fun with," Holly replied in a fond tone.

Lindsay couldn't believe she'd heard that correctly. "Your mother is Daphne Mills? The movie star?"

"Retired movie star," Holly confirmed. "These days, everyone just calls her D."

From nowhere, a little boy appeared and asked, "Can I take your coat?"

"This is our son, Chase," Holly explained, ruffling his mop of brown hair in a motherly gesture. "Chase, this is Lindsay Holland. She's going to be working at the forge with Uncle Brian."

"Cool!" he approved, flashing a gap-toothed grin. "It's gonna be awesome when he finishes it and can start making stuff. Have you seen the things he's got sketched out to make?"

She slid her new boss an accusing look. "No. He didn't tell me about any of that."

"I hate to brag," Brian said, echoing his comment at the bakery with an innocent expression that did nothing to mask the mischievous glimmer in his eyes.

Picking up on his bright mood, she laughed. "Since when? You really need to come up with a line I haven't already heard."

"I'll work on that," he conceded lightly.

People she'd never met were milling around the main floor of Ellie's home, exchanging stories and jokes with one another. Brian introduced her around, and she did her best to follow along. Normally, she had a steel-trap memory, but the unfamiliar names and faces blurred into a swirl of relatives she feared she'd never remember on her own.

She was grateful when he angled her away from the throng and headed back to the foyer. "Looks like Mom and Gran have outdone themselves again. Are you hungry?"

"Starving." This time last week, she hadn't been sure how long her meal money would hold out, and the stress of traveling in the winter had sapped her energy and left her too worried to eat much of anything. Now that she was settled, her appetite had finally caught up with her.

Placing his hand on her back to guide her forward, he said, "Let's get you some food, then. After that, we'll take our time filling everyone in."

"I hate to be rude to your family by ignoring them and stuffing our faces."

"Don't worry about it. They understand."

He sounded so confident about that, she decided to take him at his word. The formal dining room of Ellie's stately home had been transformed into a buffet area stocked with everything from spiral hams to platters full of roast beef. Lindsay counted four different salads, bowls of various potatoes and enough fresh-baked bread to keep a deli going for days.

The mingled scents of so much deliciousness were almost more than she could process, and she breathed it all in with a smile. "This is incredible. The inspector didn't leave until almost two. How did they manage to do so much in just a few hours?"

"Never underestimate the power of good news," Brian informed her with a chuckle. "Or a motivated bunch of Calhouns."

"I'll keep that in mind."

Moving along the buffet, they filled their plates and found a couple of chairs in a corner of the bustling living room. Some of the people she remembered, others were new to her, but they all had one thing in common.

They were having a fabulous time.

Laughing, talking, making sure the kids were more or less behaving themselves. Since Lindsay's arrival, the old house had been quiet, with only Ellie, Brian and her around to break to silence. Tonight, it was full of raucous life, and Ellie seemed to be everywhere at once, her delighted face making it clear how overjoyed she was to have so much company.

"I think Gran missed her calling," Brian mused. "She should've been a ringmaster at a circus."

"That's what I was thinking," Lindsay replied, stunned by the coincidence.

"Really?" When she nodded, he winked at her. "Great minds and all that."

"Oh, you're still an arrogant piece of work."

"Part of my charm."

He flashed her a shameless grin that made her roll her eyes. "If you say so."

Those warm blue eyes met hers so directly, her heart rate spiked into hummingbird range. She covered her reaction by sipping some of her cranberry juice. Once their unexpected connection was broken, her pulse settled back to a more normal pace. Apparently, time hadn't eroded all those old feelings, after all. The small-town boy she'd adored as a teenager still had the power to rattle her usual composure and leave her feeling slightly light-headed.

It would've been nice to know that before she accepted a job that would require being around him so much. But there was no help for that now, she reminded herself sternly. No one else in town was hiring, and she couldn't travel elsewhere to work. She'd just have to make the best of it.

Hoping she just came across as mildly interested, she said, "So, did you have a nice New Year's?"

Squinting up at the ceiling, he came back to her with a chuckle. "I was sound asleep by ten and watched the Times Square ball drop on the morning news. Exciting, huh?"

"I was in bed by nine," she confided, resting a hand on her stomach. "I guess my party days are in the past."

"Emma always hosts a kids' party at the church so parents can go out to dinner and know their little ones are having fun, too."

"How is your sister?" Lindsay asked, glancing around. "I don't see her anywhere."

Brian's expression darkened, as if a cloud had suddenly blocked out the sun. "She hasn't been feeling well, so Mom convinced her to stay home tonight."

Lindsay got the feeling there was more to the story, but she was hesitant to pry into family business. Still, he seemed so upset that she couldn't simply go on as if she hadn't noticed. "I'm sorry to hear that. Is it something serious?"

"Leukemia," he answered on a sigh so heavy, she

could almost feel the weight of his concern. "She's a real trouper, but the chemo's been tough on her."

"And everyone who loves her, I'd imagine," Lindsay added, feeling instant sympathy for what he must be going through. Brian sometimes came across as cocky and self-assured, but she knew better than most that beneath all that attitude beat a soft and generous heart. Years ago, he'd offered it to her on a platter, and out of stupidity she'd turned away from it without a second thought.

If only she'd had the sense to take what he'd tried to give her back then, her life would have turned out completely different. She had no doubt that come next New Year's Eve, Brian's business would be on firmer footing and he'd be sharing that traditional kiss with someone special. She just wished she could feel as confident about having the same for herself.

Discouraged by the thought, she tried to distract herself by buttering a flaky roll. "So, you have to tell me... what is Daphne Mills like?"

"A little flaky, but nice. She's always been real good to Sam, even before he connected with Holly. He had a tough time after he came home from the army, but he's doing well now. Daphne had a hand in that, and I'll always appreciate it."

The fondness in his tone was even more endearing than the mock boastfulness she'd heard earlier, and she felt an unfamiliar tug deep inside her. All her life, she'd longed for a family like this one, full of people who genuinely cared about each other and their neighbors. People who saw a need and pitched in wherever they could to help. That feeling of community had been missing from her vagabond existence, first with her mother and later with Jeff.

She still wanted it, she realized with a ferocity that startled her. For herself and her child, who deserved better than to grow up here and there, never truly belonging anywhere. A sudden rush of emotions threatened to swamp her, and she focused on her plate to mask them until they receded.

"Lindsay?"

The worry in Brian's voice was unmistakable, and that tug was back, a little stronger this time. Some part of her seemed to be leaning toward him, but her painful string of failures yanked her back to a more cautious— and much safer—distance.

Summoning a calm expression, she met his concerned gaze. "Yes?"

He studied her for several long moments, and she endured his assessment as calmly as she could manage with her heart doing its best to pound its way through her chest.

Finally, he broke away and stood. "I'm going in for seconds. Would you like anything?"

"No, thanks. I'm good."

He gave her one last look, then shook his head slightly before strolling back to the buffet. As she watched him go, Lindsay let out a pensive sigh.

She'd reconnected with Brian only a few days ago, and already she was having trouble viewing him as nothing other than her new boss. Working so closely with him every day was going to be a lot tougher than she'd anticipated.

Chapter Five

Brian was dead asleep when something jolted him instantly awake.

Disoriented by grogginess and the pitch black around him, he blinked in the late-January darkness, waiting for his eyes to adjust so he could figure out what he'd heard. It was 3:00 a.m., and the sound of ice pinging against the glass drew his eyes to the window. Outside, all he could see was swirling white.

After staring out for a few seconds, he noticed there was an odd quality to the snowstorm, a weird revolving light that looked vaguely familiar. Once his brain kicked in with the answer, he jumped from his bed, tugging on his snowmobiling boots and jacket before hurrying out the front door.

The wind hit him with a force that felt almost angry, and he staggered back a couple of steps before he grabbed the porch railing and managed to regain his balance. A quick glance confirmed his suspicion, that a snowplow had missed its turn and crashed headlong down the creek bank, coming to rest at an alarming angle. Brian raced toward the iconic covered bridge, which was missing several feet along one side, all the while praying for the safety of the driver in the elevated cab.

The interior dash lights were on, and Brian could see the driver slumped across the wheel, thankfully held in place by his seat belt. The truck was still running, and the steep incline made it tough to climb up the side. With some effort, he managed to haul himself up the mounting steps only to discover that the door was locked. Out of ideas, he settled for banging his fist on the window.

"Hey!" Nothing. He tried again, and this time the driver stirred slightly. Hoping for the best, Brian shouted, "I'm here to help get you out. Unlock the door!"

The man moved slowly, fumbling around with a gloved hand, trying to locate the mechanism. Electronic locks, Brian fumed silently. What a pain. In the old days, he probably could've jimmied the thing open with a crowbar.

After what felt like an eternity, he heard the telltale click of the lock releasing and grasped the handle for a good tug. It came open, but the heavy door nearly crushed him as gravity interfered with his efforts. Struggling against it and the slant of the truck, he clambered up to the wider top step and took a moment to catch his breath.

"I dunno what happened," the driver mumbled, cradling his head in one hand.

"There's a huge patch of ice back there," Brian informed him. "You must've hit it and started skidding toward the bridge. It's a good thing the creek's frozen, or you'd be soaking wet besides. Can you reach over and shut off the engine?"

"Yeah." The truck went silent, and he lifted his head

to peer out the windshield. "This storm turned out to be a lot worse than they were predicting, and the roads are really bad. I need to get back to work."

"Hate to break this to you, man, but that's the creek bank." Brian pointed through the windshield to illustrate his point. "This truck's done for tonight."

When it dawned on him that he was truly stuck, the guy let out a low groan. "Guess I better call in and get someone else out here."

He reached for the dash radio, but he was still a little dazed and missed the switch. Brian took charge and was relieved to hear a voice he recognized on the other end of the line.

"Alan, this is Brian Calhoun. One of your trucks just went in the creek. I'm here with—" he checked the guy's badge "—Darren, and he's basically okay but definitely needs to see a doctor. I'm taking him over to the cottage at the forge, so can you call an ambulance and the sheriff for us?"

"All our EMTs are out on the highway, but I'll send a couple certified volunteers to your place. Darren?"

"Yeah?"

"Don't worry about anything other than getting to a doctor, son. We'll cover the roads till you're cleared to come back to work. Okay?"

The young man nodded, and Brian translated, then thanked Alan and signed off. After that, he wasted no time in helping Darren from his seat. Now that the engine was off, the truck was quickly cooling down, and he wasn't keen on either of them turning into a Popsicle while they waited for medical help.

Between his still-dazed companion and the crazy angle of the truck, it was slow going, but Brian finally lowered them both safely to the ground. Once they were in the relative warmth of his house, Darren looked up and whispered a heartfelt "Thanks."

Darren was sore more than anything, but Brian was still concerned because the driver had been nearly unconscious when he'd first found him. After they shed their winter gear, he walked his guest into his small living room.

"Have a seat," he said, tossing a jumble of dirty clothes onto the floor to make space on the couch, "but don't fall asleep."

"Okay."

Brian tossed a couple of logs onto the coals and stirred up the fire. "Want some coffee?"

"That'd be great."

The pass-through from the kitchen allowed Brian to keep an eye on Darren while he threw together a snack of spray cheese and some crackers he found in the back of a nearly bare cupboard. He really needed to do some grocery shopping, he thought as he went back into the quickly warming room with a middle-of-the-night snack.

"Crackers might be stale," he warned with a chuckle to lighten the mood. "I thought the cheese might cover that up."

"Thanks." Darren downed one in a single bite, then made a face and chased the food with a long swallow of coffee. He didn't say anything, but Brian could guess what had prompted the reaction.

"Cheese is spoiled, right?" His poor visitor nodded, and he grimaced. "Sorry about that. Like your night hasn't been bad enough without me trying to poison you."

"I should be the one apologizing, yanking you out of bed during a blizzard."

"No problem. I grew up here, so this kinda weather doesn't faze me."

While they waited, he kept Darren talking, in part to pass the time and also to make sure he didn't nod off. Just in case he had a concussion, Brian didn't want to take any chances. Before long, an enormous diesel pickup truck sporting a blue emergency light on the dash emerged from the storm to park in front of the porch.

When Brian chuckled, Darren gave him a quizzical look. "What's so funny?"

"It's my dad, Steve. My parents live over in Waterford, but he must've picked up the call on his scanner and started driving."

"He was worried about you," Darren commented with a droopy smile. "That's nice."

In the years he'd been away from his map-dot hometown, Brian had become accustomed to the anonymity of living in Portsmouth. On a night like tonight, it was comforting to be reminded that even though he was all grown up, his father was still watching out for him. "Yeah, it is. I'll be right back."

He met Dad and his buddy Warren at the door and was promptly hauled into one of Steve Calhoun's trademark bear hugs.

"Scared the life outta me," he muttered, giving Brian a mild shove that was eased by a smile. Looking over at the sofa, he added, "What's the story?"

"Ask him yourself, but go easy. His name's Darren, and he's still a little wonky."

"Gotcha."

The two older men approached casually, introducing themselves as if they were all meeting each other at a restaurant instead of after a frightening crash. A quick assessment of Darren's condition brought up some somber looks, but Brian noticed that they were careful not to alarm him.

"All right, then," Dad announced as he stood up. "It'll be a haul, so we'd best get moving. If you've got folks to contact, you can do that on the way. I don't recommend them driving anywhere until the storm breaks, but tell them you'll be at Waterford Memorial."

It was more of an order than a suggestion, and Darren wisely nodded. "Yes, sir."

"And you," he added, pointing at Brian, "call your mother for me. Tell her we'll be a while because the bridge is out of commission so we have to go upstream to the commercial truck crossing. That back road hasn't been plowed yet, so it'll be slow going. I'll be home soon as I can."

"Got it. Drive careful."

After another quick hug, they were gone.

Alone in his house again, Brian called his mom and delivered the message she'd obviously been anxiously waiting to hear. After assuring her that he was all in one piece, he hung up and stared out toward the bridge. He couldn't see it, but he couldn't believe he hadn't noticed earlier that the crash had left it too damaged for Dad to use on the way into town. Then again, he'd been focused on the man inside the huge truck that had been clinging to the bank.

His eventful early morning finally caught up with him, and he stretched out on the couch, letting out a weary sigh. Just as he was falling asleep, a horrible thought jerked him awake again.

The covered bridge that led into Liberty Creek was more than a quaint throwback to another time. It had been built shortly after the forge to make it easier for people to access the town, and it functioned that way even now. The secondary crossing his father had mentioned was three miles from the center of the village, and while it worked perfectly well, it redirected traffic away from the charming square and boutique shops that held such appeal for visitors from spring through the end of the autumn colors season.

Without the main bridge, the upcoming tourist season might suffer. How much was anyone's guess, but the local economy—like so many other places—was already on shaky ground. Any dip could be disastrous for the businesses that counted on increased income during the milder months to carry them through the leaner times the rest of the year. One of those businesses was Liberty Creek Forge.

Brian wasn't usually one for doom and gloom scenarios, but as he stared at the hand-hewn beams in the ceiling, it occurred to him that despite all his efforts, his new venture might be over before it had begun.

Figuring he'd never get to sleep now, he pulled on his winter gear again and fought his way through the howling wind to the bridge. Ice stung any skin that wasn't covered, but he gritted his teeth and kept going because he had to know—for certain—just how bad the situation was.

He got there just as an oversize wrecker was pulling in to rescue the plow from its precarious spot. As the mechanics attached a tow hook and began dragging the snowplow from its precarious position, it reminded Brian of an enormous fish being reeled in on a line. Deciding the lack of sleep was messing with his mind, he turned away and trudged through knee-deep snow, retracing the path of the runaway plow.

And there, at the other end, he got his answer.

The front third of the bridge was now lying on the ice below, leaving behind sturdy concrete support piers that had stood for generations but now held up nothing. Several of the oak trusses had collapsed, and sections of roof and decking were scattered over the frozen creek like a child's building toys.

Stunned but not surprised, he took one last look at the carnage and went home.

"So," Lindsay asked as she put on the wool maternity coat that had mysteriously shown up on the rack in Ellie's entryway, "who should I thank for this lovely new coat?"

"Holly must have dropped it off earlier."

Her gracious hostess busied herself finding her gloves, neatly avoiding Lindsay's gaze.

"I don't think so," Lindsay said, muting her laughter as she fingered the white tag dangling from one of the buttons. "It still has the tag on it."

Ellie gave her a guilty look, then fessed up. "All right, you caught me. Brian wanted to get a warmer coat that fit you better, but he didn't know what style you'd like. He asked me to pick one up and keep it quiet. If it makes a difference to you, it was on sale."

Lindsay had noticed his disapproval whenever she put on the too-small coat she'd been wearing. She didn't know why he wanted to keep his generosity a secret.

In their better days, Jeff had loved to crow about how much he could afford to spend on her, and she'd almost forgotten that there were guys who didn't share that unappealing quality.

But in the interest of standing on her own, she didn't feel comfortable accepting the gift. "I'll get the receipt from you later so I know how much to pay him back. In the meantime, how do these town meetings work? When Mom and I lived here, we never went to any."

The woman she considered her fairy godmother replied, "Normally, we meet the first Thursday of each month. But with the bridge emergency, our assistant mayor called one for tonight."

Speaking of calling, Lindsay still couldn't believe that Brian had canceled work for today. His explanation—vague and unsettling—had been that he just wasn't up to it after his eventful night, but he'd pay her for the day since it wasn't her fault. While she was grateful for the opportunity to rest, she couldn't help but be worried about him. He was by nature as sturdy as granite and twice as stubborn.

The forge was now cleared for full-on production, and she'd expected him to be hard at work filling his backlog of orders when she arrived at the office. For him to retreat this way, there must be something terribly wrong.

"Have you heard from Brian today?" she asked, hoping she sounded casual about it.

"Just that he'd be at the meeting tonight. Why?"

"Just curious."

Ellie didn't seem worried, so Lindsay did her best to shrug off the feeling that something was amiss with him. Apparently, she was losing her skill for masking her emotions, because Ellie turned to her with a frown.

"Is something bothering you, dear?"

Lindsay couldn't lie to this kind, generous woman who'd offered her a safe harbor from the hurricane that had engulfed her life. Grimacing, she confessed, "He didn't sound right to me, I guess. Like something was on his mind, but he didn't want to mention it to me."

"Or me," the grandmotherly woman said, her frown deepening. "Now that he's officially in business, I can't imagine what might be troubling him."

Lindsay felt awful for giving Ellie something to fret about, and she forced a smile. "It's probably just my imagination. It tends to run away with me these days."

"That comes with the territory when you're about to become a mother. There's a lot more to worry about when you're responsible for a helpless little soul."

She'd deftly summed up the emotional weight that Lindsay had been feeling lately, and it was reassuring to know that what she was experiencing wasn't unusual. Feeling a bit more upbeat than she had before, she stepped onto the front porch and waited for Ellie to lock the door.

The storm that had blown through seemed to have swept all the clouds away, and the evening air was balmy for late January in New England. Since the meeting was at the church only a few doors down, they decided to leave the car at home and walk. Splinters of ice mixed into the snow glittered beneath the vintage streetlights, giving the charming town a snow-globe effect.

After spending years schlepping from one cramped city apartment to another, Liberty Creek had a dignified grace that Lindsay didn't realize she'd been missing until she saw it again. So much had gone on in the years she'd been away, it was nice to know that there was still a tiny corner of the world where things remained the way they'd always been.

When they reached Liberty Creek Chapel, light spilled from the tall stained-glass windows onto a parking lot that was jammed to near capacity. People were climbing the steps to the double front doors that led into the entryway. Greeting each other with handshakes and plenty of laughter, you'd have thought they were filing in for a party instead of an emergency town meeting. When she shared her observation with Ellie, the older woman laughed.

"Oh, honey, we'll be fine. We'll hear what's going on, then come up with a plan to get through it. This town hasn't survived all this time by accident. We don't stand around wringing our hands when trouble comes knocking. We roll up our sleeves and get to work."

When she was younger, Lindsay hadn't appreciated the can-do attitude of the residents of this village tucked into the woods of New Hampshire. Now she admired it very much, and as they went up the steps together, she said, "Maybe there's something I can do to help."

"I wouldn't doubt it," Ellie approved, giving her arm a quick squeeze.

They hung their coats in the vestibule and paused outside the open doors for a moment. Inside, the place was standing room only, but there was a cheerful, energetic vibe that drew Lindsay forward in spite of being a virtual stranger here. Near the middle of the crowd, she noticed a movement and was pleased to find Brian standing at the end of a pew, waving to them.

"He looks completely worn-out," Ellie murmured as

they made their way to the seats he'd saved for them. "I can see why you were worried."

Lindsay could think of only one thing that would cause him to so quickly crash from the high of passing his inspection and finally being allowed to work on his projects the way he wanted.

The forge.

Her heart thudded to a stop when she realized that if his business failed, she was out of a job. She'd put all her hopes into remaining here until the baby was born. Now, just as she was beginning to feel more comfortable about her situation, the possibility of all that evaporating made her sick inside. A chill crept up her spine, and she shivered despite the warm air inside the packed sanctuary.

"You okay?" Brian asked, frowning in obvious concern.

"Sure," she replied, willing it to be true. "How are you?"

"Fine."

Ellie gave him a long suspicious look but didn't say anything while she took her seat next to Holly. The whole family was there, and Lindsay happily disappeared into the midst of the Calhoun clan. It kept her from wondering if anyone was staring at her, and she welcomed the distraction from brooding over her suddenly precarious circumstances.

Tugging the sleeve of his faded flannel shirt, she waited for him to look her way. Leaning closer so she could speak quietly, she said, "Thank you for the coat. It's just my style, and very warm."

He glanced at his grandmother, who held up her hands in a "what can you do?" gesture. Coming back to Lindsay, he chuckled. "You're welcome."

"I'll pay you back," she promised, proud that she'd actually have the money to do it soon. "As long as you don't mind setting up an installment plan."

He seemed to be confused by her offer, and she fully expected him to refuse. Then, to her astonishment, he nodded. "However you wanna do it is fine with me."

"Thanks. It means a lot to me that I can take care of myself."

"I know."

Understanding showed in his features, and the blue in his eyes twinkled with something she hadn't gotten much of recently. Respect.

He looked away when a middle-aged woman stopped beside him. "Are you Brian Calhoun?"

"Yes, ma'am," he responded, smiling as he got to his feet. "Can I help you?"

"I'm Mary Peters, and I wanted to thank you personally for rescuing Darren last night. I'm a widow, and he's my only child, so he's all I have. If you hadn't gone out into that storm to rescue him, there's no telling how long he would've been out in that terrible cold all by himself."

She reached out to take one of his hands in both of her much smaller ones, and he gently rested his other over top of them. "I'm sure he would've managed just fine, but I'm glad I could help. How's he doing?"

"They kept him overnight at the hospital, but he's home now. He's got whiplash and a nasty headache, but the doctor said there shouldn't be any lasting effects. My neighbor's keeping an eye on him, because he wanted me to come and see what this meeting's all about. Do you know?"

Something Lindsay couldn't define flashed through

Brian's shadowed eyes, but it vanished as quickly as it had appeared. "I guess we'll know soon enough. Please tell Darren I'll say a prayer for him to get back on his feet real soon."

"Bless you," she whispered, beaming up at him before making her way back to her seat.

Lindsay couldn't help noticing the easy way the two of them talked about prayers and blessings. Most of the people she knew weren't the least bit religious, and some of them even doubted that God existed at all. Her own chaotic upbringing had left little room for belief in things she couldn't verify for herself. Sadly, even some that had seemed tangible to her had proven to be less than trustworthy.

"Earth to Lindsay," Brian teased, waving a hand in front of her face. "You still with us?"

"Just thinking."

"Yeah, I figured. What about?"

She hesitated, then decided that there was no harm in sharing her thoughts. "How nice it is to have something to believe in."

"Like God, you mean?"

"Yes. How do you manage to trust someone when you can't prove they exist?"

Even to her own ears, the question sounded childish, and she waited for him to laugh at her. Instead, he gave her a smile tinged with understanding. "That's a good question. I guess that's why they call it faith."

"I've never had much of that," she confessed with a sigh.

"I know."

He didn't say anything more, but his smile took on a sad quality, as if he was remembering the troubled girl she'd been in high school. And, out of the blue, she heard herself ask, "Why were you always so nice to me?"

"Because you deserved it."

A bit of the affection she used to see in those blue depths sparkled out at her now, and she leaned closer, unable to resist the comforting feel of him sitting beside her. "What about now?"

She regretted the question before it even left her lips, and fortunately she was saved from hearing the answer by the sound of a gavel banging on the tall wooden lectern.

"All right, then. Let's get started!" the tall white-haired man shouted. In just a few seconds, the din receded, and he continued. "Now, for anyone who's new here, I'm Hal Rogers, assistant mayor of this crazy little town. Our esteemed mayor is off globetrotting, so I'll be handling this in his absence. But since I'm not an expert on our current situation, I'll turn over the floor to Alan Kerwin, superintendent of our highway department."

A large man stepped up to the microphone and got right to business. "Well, folks, I'm afraid I've got some bad news. The temporary closing of the main bridge coming into town is gonna last longer than we'd like. A structural engineer came out this afternoon to do a thorough examination, and his recommendation is that we replace the whole structure, from one bank straight across to the other."

There were several gasps, and a horrified buzzing zipped through the crowd like a swarm of agitated wasps. He let that go on for a few seconds, then held up his hands to quiet everyone down. "I know it's a tough blow, but there's no way around it. The supporting piers are sound as ever, but everything else has to be torn out and replaced. I'm sure I don't have to tell you that's gonna be a big, expensive job."

"How big and expensive?" someone asked.

He named a figure that paled more than a few faces, then grimaced before going on. "There's more. Because this winter's been so bad, our highway fund is already running in the red. We won't have the money for repairs until property taxes are collected in June, and even then it'll be snug. I realize that will impact our tourist traffic, but there's no way around it."

Brian heaved a deep sigh, and Lindsay realized his worst fears had just been confirmed. The charming little town relied heavily on visitors to keep its fragile economy going. If that took a hit, the local businesses and the dozens of residents who worked for them would suffer. The question was: How much?

"There must be something we can do to raise the money," Ellie called out, looking around at her neighbors with a determined expression. "Does anyone have any ideas for raising a lot of money in a short period of time?"

Several people chimed in with suggestions from staging various auctions to selling off a significant chunk of community-owned property. Inspiration struck, and Lindsay held up her hand to be recognized. When Hal formally recognized her, she took a deep breath to steady her voice. "Valentine's Day is coming up, and folks are always looking for something fun to do this time of year. What about putting together a Sweetheart Dance? We could advertise in all the towns around here, to bring in more people. If the proceeds go into the bridge fund, that would really help."

To her right, she sensed Brian staring at her as if she'd grown another head. To her great relief, others reacted more positively, and her idea was quickly seconded and affirmed by an overwhelming majority vote.

Chuckling, Brian leaned in to murmur, "You realize this means you're in charge of it, right?"

That hadn't occurred to her, and a quick glance at Ellie got her a confirming nod. Reaching over, she gave Lindsay's arm a reassuring squeeze. "Don't worry, honey. We'll all lend a hand. Won't we, Brian?"

"I don't know, Gran. That's really not my kinda thing."

"Fixing the bridge before spring is everyone's thing," she informed him sternly, her stony expression challenging him to dispute her logic.

He didn't even bother trying. Lindsay smothered a grin, even as she made a mental note to find out how Ellie had perfected that look. She had a feeling it just might come in handy someday.

Chapter Six

"Then you click here." Lindsay continued their computer lesson by demonstrating what she meant. "And you can enter your expenses for the month. I've set up a bunch of categories that are appropriate for this kind of business, so your costs can be classified as anything from raw materials to office equipment."

"Like this fancy new laptop you ordered the other day?" he asked with one of those maddening grins that held as much sarcasm as humor.

"Oh, let it go, Brian. I got it on sale. This is far from the latest model, but it has everything you'll need to keep the business on track."

"And more. You really think I'm gonna remember all these bookkeeping sessions you're torturing me with?"

She flashed him a sympathetic smile. "I know it's a lot, and you're not the only person in the world who's intimidated by technology. I promise that with some patience and practice, you'll be an expert."

"I gotta be honest… I've been picturing something more like this." Pausing, he cleared his throat and took a blank sheet of paper from the new printer on the desk.

Handing it to her, he said, "Lindsay, I just bought myself a nice red Ferrari. Here's the receipt."

Because he was still just about irresistible as ever, she decided to play along. "And this is a business expense how?"

He cocked his head, doing a good impression of someone who was seriously considering her question. "You're the brains of this outfit, sweetheart. I'm the muscle."

Oh, he was a real piece of work. "How is it you just managed to compliment us both in the same breath?"

"It's a gift."

The mischievous twinkle in his eyes made her laugh, and the warmth that nudged into her heart felt so good, she never wanted to stop. Suddenly, a sharp pain stabbed her side, making her gasp in dismay.

Before she even registered that he'd moved, Brian was on his knees in front of her, his jaw set in concern. "Lindsay, are you okay?"

She couldn't speak, so she held up a forefinger in a wordless request for him to give her a second. Once the cramp began to recede, she slowly inhaled and let the breath out the way she'd learned from one of her pregnancy books. Then, taking pity on him, she forced a shaky smile. "Fine. Just a pang."

"How often do you get these 'pangs'?" he demanded.

"Not often." He gave her a doubtful look, and she rolled her eyes in defeat. "Okay, they started about a week ago and have happened a few times since then. Happy?"

"I will be," he replied, striding over to get their coats from the rack by the door. "As soon as you see a doctor who gives you a thorough check-up and says you and the baby are all right. There's a women's clinic not far from here. It's free for folks who need a little help."

Meaning her, she realized grimly. This time last year, she had a good job, a decent place to live and a fairly reliable car. What on earth had happened to her? After a lot of soul-searching, she'd come to the conclusion that her current predicament wasn't Jeff's fault alone. She'd done plenty to sabotage her own life, and now she was dealing with the consequences. She wouldn't compound the problem by allowing her child to suffer for her mistakes.

"All right, but I need to bring this," she replied, closing the laptop and sliding it into its protective case.

"Really?"

"I just got this thing configured the way I want it, and I'm not leaving it here so someone can waltz through your crack security and snag it. I'm not letting it out of my sight."

"Fine, but let me carry it for you. And for the record, that lock might not be new, but it's as sturdy as ever."

Tiring of their latest battle of wills, she gave in. "Whatever."

He helped her into her coat, and then she turned to face him. Worry for her clouded his handsome face, and she couldn't help admiring a man who could feel such compassion for someone who'd once treated him like dirt. "Thank you."

"You're welcome. Now, let's go."

Brian kept his four-wheel drive near the speed limit and distracted her with small talk about the business, but Lindsay could hear the nervousness running beneath the surface of his deep voice. When they arrived at the clinic, he wasted no time getting her inside and checked in. Then he pulled the kind of stunt that she would always think of as "The Brian."

Leaning on the top of the reception desk, he flashed one of his notorious knee-weakening grins at the poor woman who'd been ogling the tall, well-built blacksmith since the moment they walked in. "Miss Holland really needs to see someone right away. Is there any way you can help us out with that?"

The woman's eyes flicked to Lindsay and then back to him. "Your relationship to the patient?"

"She's my office manager."

Technically, that was true, but Lindsay felt a little twinge of regret that he'd so easily classified her as nothing more than his employee. But she recognized his tactic as an attempt to get her admitted more quickly, so she did her best to ignore her reaction to it. After all, it wasn't any different from her flirting with the environmental inspector to get on his good side. So why did it bother her so much?

"Hold on and I'll check to see who's available." After a quick back-and-forth on the phone, she hung up and angled a subtle look down the hallway. Very quietly, she said, "One of our nurses can see you now in room four."

Lindsay thanked her and moved away from the desk. To her amazement, Brian asked, "Want me to come with you?"

"No, I'm fine," she answered reflexively. When he strolled into the waiting room and took a seat, she wished she'd been more honest with him. Because as she went down that sterile hallway to be examined by a stranger, she felt tiny and vulnerable. And very much alone.

Fortunately, a nurse whose name tag identified her as Karen was waiting for her, so she didn't have time for a pity party. After stepping on the scale, she followed Karen into a small but brightly painted room and managed to get up on the exam table.

"You're a little on the light side, considering how far along you are," the nurse told her in a motherly tone. Despite the clinical garb, Lindsay found the woman's personable demeanor reassuring, and for the first time in weeks, she felt as if things were actually going to be okay.

"I've been traveling," she explained, purposefully keeping it vague. Nice as Karen was, Lindsay had no intention of spilling her guts to someone she didn't know. "Getting here took me longer than I expected, and it was kind of hard on my stomach."

"Does that mean you're settled in now?"

Well, she had a job and people who cared about what happened to her. In her mind, that was a definite step up. "More or less."

"Let's work on making that a yes," Karen suggested with a sympathetic expression, reaching into a drawer for a large bottle that she handed over. "Take these vitamins every day, and if your stomach is still off, try smaller meals and snacks throughout the day. That way, you and the baby will get what you need and you'll have less digestive problems."

Her prenatal vitamins were one of the things she'd continued using, even when she'd had to scrape together change to buy them. But she understood that Karen was trying to be helpful, so she simply nodded. "Okay."

"Did you have a sonogram at any point?"

This time, Lindsay shook her head, feeling like the worst mother-to-be in history. "I didn't know I needed one."

"Often, someone as young and generally healthy as you doesn't. But it's good to be on the safe side. We have the equipment here, and we offer free scans to all our patients."

Translation: when you're dead broke, we'll pay for your test. Lindsay mentally cringed at the implication, but she recognized that she couldn't allow her pride to jeopardize the health of her baby. Her son or daughter was all she had in the world, and there was nothing she wouldn't do for this child. "I think that makes sense. Thank you."

"No worries," Karen assured her briskly. "I think there's a patient in the room now, so you might have to wait a few minutes. Is there someone here with you?"

Brian was out front, and knowing him, he'd already charmed half the women in the waiting room. Over the years, his rangy build had filled in a bit, and in his flannel shirt and faded jeans he had the look of a lean lumberjack. Much as she'd liked him back in high school, Lindsay remembered wishing he was more polished, maybe on his way to college or up some corporate ladder.

Then again, she thought wryly, when she met him, Jeff had claimed to be on that kind of path, and he'd disappointed her time after time. Pushing the pointless reminiscing aside, she replied, "A friend drove me here, but I'm not sure he'd want to see this."

She braced herself for a pitying look, but Karen simply smiled. "It's your call, of course, but if he cared enough to bring you here, I'd imagine he's the supportive type. Do you want me to go out and ask him?"

"I guess it can't hurt."

"Then I'll be right back. We can work around your

clothes, so go ahead and get dressed." She patted Lindsay's shoulder on the way out, leaving her alone with more unsettling thoughts that she'd rather not explore right now. Or ever.

Thankfully, only a couple of minutes later someone knocked on the door. "Come in."

When Brian peered into the exam room, Lindsay was so flabbergasted that she blurted, "You came."

"Sure I came." Stepping inside, he let the door fall closed and eyed her as if she'd gone completely off her rocker. "Why wouldn't I?"

Jeff had never exhibited the slightest interest in having a family. In hindsight, that should have been a warning to her about how things between them would end. "I'm pretty sure Jeff wouldn't have, and he was the father."

The warmth left Brian's eyes, and they glittered like shards of glass. "I told you before, you're better off without him. You and the baby both are."

The way his voice softened when he referred to her child made Lindsay's eyes mist with gratitude. He could have just dropped her off at the clinic and picked her up when she was finished. But he'd insisted on staying, even though this was probably the last thing he'd envisioned doing today. "Yes, you did. I appreciate you saying that."

"I also meant it. Both times."

"I know." Her voice cracked a little, and she blinked away tears that were threatening to spill over.

"Aw, man." Glancing around, he found some tissues and handed the box to her. "Are you okay?"

Not trusting herself to speak normally, Lindsay nodded, dabbing at her eyes while she furiously tried to pull herself together. Brian had been nothing but kind to her since she showed up at the forge, and the last thing she wanted to do was repay his generosity with blubbering.

"I'm fine." Shaking off the lingering bout of vulnerability, she sat up straighter and forced a smile. "Pregnant women get emotional for no reason sometimes. No biggie."

"I'd say you've got plenty of reason." He seemed ready to add something more, then seemed to think better of it and clamped his mouth shut around a grimace.

"Go ahead, Brian. If you've got something to say, just spit it out. It can't be any worse than what I've been saying to myself for the past few months."

"Back when he lived here, I always hated that guy," he growled, his features hardening dangerously. "I just could never figure out why."

A question that had haunted her for years bubbled to the surface, but Lindsay hesitated. Did she really want to know the answer? After debating with herself for a few seconds, she finally decided that she had to settle things between them once and for all. "What about me?"

His expression softened immediately, and he shook his head with a wry grin. "I tried to hate you, but I could never quite manage it. Once I got over you skipping town that way, I realized it never would've worked for us because we wanted different things out of life. I'm a feet-on-the-ground kinda guy, and you wanted to fly. It just would've been nice if you'd told me you were going."

Yes, it would have, Lindsay thought morosely. Brian was such a good guy, and she'd truly cared about him. Maybe even loved him, but she couldn't say for certain. She'd loved Jeff, and look where that had gotten her.

Some people didn't do well with intense emotions, and more than once she'd wondered if she was one of them.

But regret was something she was well acquainted with, and she said, "I'm sorry, Brian. I wish there was some way I could make it up to you."

To her surprise, he turned the somber conversation around with twinkling eyes. "Take good care of yourself and this baby, and help me get my business organized, and we'll call it even."

"Deal."

They shook to seal their bargain just as Karen knocked and opened the door for a technician wheeling in a machine that looked capable of talking to someone in outer space. The young woman efficiently hooked everything up and then turned to look from Lindsay to Brian. "Ready?"

A panicked look flew across his face, and he put up his hands as he took a big step back. "I'm not the father. I'm just here for moral support."

He was awfully quick to correct the mistake, Lindsay noted wryly. Not that she could blame him.

"You don't want to see?" the tech asked him.

Lindsay waited for him to answer, curious to hear what he'd say. He'd been raised in a large, loving family but didn't yet have one of his own. It suggested to her that he liked his bachelor's life and didn't have any immediate plans for trading in his imaginary Ferrari for a minivan.

Then, to her astonishment, he stopped his backpedaling and slid a questioning look her way. "Whatta you think?"

"It's fine with me."

The tech coated Lindsay's stomach with gel and fiddled around with the scanning end of the machine until she apparently found the right spot. Pointing to the monitor with her other hand, she announced, "There you go."

Lindsay squinted at the blob on the screen, trying to find a human shape in the grainy image. Just when she was about to give up, a tiny limb moved, as if the little person inside her was waving. Her heart shot into her throat, and she asked, "Is that an arm?"

"Yes, it is."

"Whoa," Brian murmured, edging in for a closer look. "How cool is that?"

"Very," Lindsay agreed. Then a wild thought popped into her head, and she asked the tech, "Can you tell if it's a boy or a girl?"

"Yes, I can." Glancing at Brian, she asked, "Do you both want to know?"

"I'm not the father," he reminded her. "If Lindsay wants to know, go ahead and tell her."

"Then it's a girl. Ten fingers and toes, and a good size for this stage. At this point, everything looks good."

"At this point?" A chill shivered down Lindsay's spine, as if someone had tossed ice water on her joyful mood. "What do you mean by that?"

"Healthy children aren't born by chance," Karen said gently. "You have to take excellent care of yourself and get consistent medical attention to ensure that the rest of your pregnancy and the delivery go as well as possible. This little cutie is counting on you."

She nodded at the flickering image on the screen, and Lindsay followed the prompt to look at the monitor.

Her daughter.

Those two simple words settled into her heart with a weight she hadn't felt before. Since discovering that

she was pregnant, she'd accepted that it was her job
to give her baby the best start she possibly could. But
somehow, seeing her in person for the first time gave
Lindsay's situation a whole new spin that she couldn't
quite put into words. Her heart was overjoyed that the
child was doing well, but her mind careened from one
worry to the next, even while she recognized that most
of them wouldn't even apply to her for months.

Before her imagination galloped off with her good
sense, she firmly pushed her fear aside and focused
on the present. She and the baby were doing well, and
thanks to Brian she'd have the means to make sure that
continued.

For now, that was all that mattered.

Brian had been working day and night for months
to get the old ironworks into some semblance of working order. His revenue stream was more like a trickle,
and he knew it would take some serious commitment
from him to improve it. But today, Lindsay's emergency
had distracted him from his own problems, and he realized that taking care of her was a lot more important
than finishing a garden sculpture for a customer who
wouldn't be using it until spring.

Because he wasn't much of a cook, he stopped in at
the bakery and fell on Gran's mercy. After giving her
the quick version of their morning, he got the response
he was after.

After hugging Lindsay, she ordered, "You two sit
down and I'll bring you something to eat."

"It doesn't make sense to take the entire afternoon
off," Lindsay protested as they found an empty table.
"We both have a lot to do at the forge."

She had a point there, he acknowledged, but he questioned whether she'd be comfortable enough in the makeshift office there. "I'll tell you what—we'll ask Gran if we can use her office. It's warmer, and she's got a nice, cushy desk chair like the one you bookmarked online."

"You saw that?"

"It was hard to miss. I also noticed that you marked the page for Waterford University," he added in a casual tone so she wouldn't scold him for snooping. "Are you looking at taking some psychology classes after the baby's born?"

"Well, maybe," she allowed, touching the screen to show him what she'd been reading. "At your celebration party, Holly told me that she's in their interior design program, and she loves it. She was able to put together a schedule for online and on-campus courses that gives her time at home and at school."

"Sounds perfect for you," he approved, tapping the top edge of the laptop screen. "I know we bought this for the business, but you're welcome to use it anytime."

"I'm not sure about college."

"Then use it for whatever, until you can afford to get one for yourself."

She gave him a dubious look, then a shadow of that sassy grin wrinkled the corner of her mouth. "You're the boss."

"Just keep telling yourself that, sweetheart," he teased. "We'll get along fine."

A bit of that old spark glittered in her eyes, alerting him that some of her spirit was coming back. "Not if you keep calling me 'sweetheart.'"

"Got it."

While they ate, her comment about him being the boss rattled around in his brain. Being the middle child of three, he'd always had the luxury of doing his own thing. Big brother Sam was the leader, even before he joined the army and became a Ranger before being discharged with honors. Their younger sister, Emma, was the princess, which left Brian the role of easygoing drifter. He'd never been in charge of anything before, and now that he had an employee, the monumental task he'd taken on had a lot more weight to it.

Sopping up gravy with her bread, Lindsay told him, "I've been wanting to ask you something for a while now." When he motioned for her to go on, she said, "I'm dying to know how you ended up living at the forge."

"My lease ran out at the end of last year, and I figured rather than wasting money on more rent and gas for my truck, I'd cut down on my commute by moving into the old cottage at the ironworks. There's a bathroom and a small kitchen, which I don't really need because Gran keeps me fed. It's not much to look at, and the furnace isn't all that reliable. But there's a fireplace, so it works for me."

"Is it safe for you to live there?" Lindsay asked, frowning in obvious concern.

"Building inspector okayed it when he gave me the go-ahead on the rehab. Beyond getting some inventory on the shelves, my biggest hurdle has been the environmental regulations for running a coal-fired forge in a business district. The air-scrubbing equipment wiped out most of my savings, but now that it's installed and approved, I'm glad I did it."

"Why did you decide to go to that extreme?" Lindsay asked in a practical tone at odds with his memory of a careless girl who'd always drifted from one thing to the next. "You could install a modern system and still make things the old-fashioned way."

"I want it to be as authentic as possible, so it runs the way it did when the Calhouns first started out. Once we get to tourist season, the ironworks will be crawling with visitors, and I want them to get the full-on experience. Jordan puts on live demonstrations at Renaissance fairs, and he does twice the business of guys who just bring everything in already finished. Folks love sparks and fire."

"Sparks and fire," Lindsay echoed, teasing a napkin from the holder on the table. "I need to write that down for the website. Do you have a pen?"

"Whatta you think?"

She laughed, and it struck him that he was beginning to hear that more often now. "I think this is like math class, when I had to bring extra pencils for you."

"Here you go, honey," his grandmother said, handing over one of the pens that she kept in the front pocket of her flour-covered apron. "Knowing Brian, you'll need plenty of office supplies before you can get anything done."

"That means a trip to the nearest mall, I guess," Lindsay complained, wiggling the feet she had propped on a chair in front of her.

She didn't sound as enthused about that as most women he'd known would have, and it occurred to him that his new office manager was beginning to run out of steam. He could either put it off—and lose another day of work time—or come up with an alternative.

Inspiration struck when a sign on the wall caught his attention.

We don't have internet in here. Talk to each other.

"We can get a lotta this stuff online. Gran, I know you don't like folks using the web connection here, but could you make an exception for us? We'll work in your office so no one sees us."

She gave him a suspicious look, but the fondness twinkling in her eyes kind of ruined the effect. "If I tell you the code, you have to promise you'll keep it to yourselves. I'm not running one of those newfangled internet cafés, and I don't want people sitting in here with their noses tucked into their chests, staring at their phones."

"Scout's honor," he replied, holding up his hand.

"You quit the Scouts in second grade, so I hardly think that applies."

"Really?" Lindsay asked. "Why?"

"I didn't like being told what to do and how to do it."

"I know what you mean."

"So," he commented, rocking his chair back on its legs because he knew it drove Gran crazy, "we're just a couple of rebels."

That got him a half smile. "I guess so."

"You're quite the pair," Gran said. She leaned in to whisper the supersecret code to him, then added, "The after-school snacks should be done soon, and I'll bring you something for dessert. And a nice glass of milk for your little one," she added, patting Lindsay's shoulder in the sweet gesture she used with people from two years old to eighty.

As she headed back into the kitchen, Lindsay watched her go and then sighed. "Your grandmother is the absolute best. I don't know what would've happened to me and the baby if she didn't take us in the way she did."

"Yeah, she's something else." Standing, he motioned her ahead of him. "Ready to get to work?"

Laughing again, she pointed in the other direction. "Bathroom first."

The way she said it made him chuckle. "Guess I'm gonna have to get used to that, huh?"

"I'll try to make sure I'm worth the trouble."

The way she ducked her head alerted him that he'd inadvertently pushed one of her buttons, and he frowned. She sidled past him, and he reached out to gently catch her arm. She glowered up at him and jerked her arm free. The defiant motion told him more than he needed to know about what had happened to her, and he vowed that if he ever met up with Jeff again, things wouldn't end well for the deadbeat father.

Striving for a calm tone, he asked, "Where'd you get the idea that you're trouble?"

"Lots of people. Ask anyone."

"I'm asking you."

"Brian, don't do this. I don't want to get into it with you."

"You mean now," he clarified, "or not ever?"

"Yes. Now can I please go to the bathroom?"

He stepped back, and she lumbered past him in what he now recognized was her top speed. So many things she'd said to him since their unexpected reunion made no sense to him, and part of him wished that she'd chosen somewhere else to go.

Another part, one he wasn't crazy about right now, was happy that she'd come back. While he understood that she hadn't returned to him personally, he liked knowing that when she found herself out of options, she thought of Liberty Creek. He understood the appeal of the quaint little town buried in the depths of New Hampshire, far from the cold, unfeeling world that had chewed him up and spit him out more times than he cared to recall.

Instinct told him that Lindsay had experienced it much the same way, and needed a safe haven to catch her breath and have her baby. After that, who knew? As unpredictable as she was beautiful, the blue-eyed gypsy that had captured his heart so long ago didn't seem to have changed all that much.

Working with her would be a challenge, given their personal history. Then again, he had a business to launch, so that should help him keep her at an appropriate distance. He wasn't a shirker, and he'd always put his best effort into whatever he did. Responsibility for someone else was new to him, and he wasn't at all certain he was ready for it. But now Lindsay and her unborn child were counting on him, even if it was only for a paycheck.

When she rejoined him, they generated a reasonable list of supplies, which she typed into the computer without looking at the keys even once. Being technologically challenged, Brian was impressed by yet another skill she had that his business desperately needed.

During a lull, she took a sip of water and then said, "I was thinking."

He chuckled. "Is that good or bad?"

"That depends on what you think of my idea."

"Okay. Shoot."

"Well, I really like the custom-order concept for the forge, because you'll only be making things you've already sold."

He appreciated the compliment, but it didn't take

a genius to see that she had something else in mind. "But?"

"I'm wondering if you could keep a small inventory of stock items that are always available. That way, someone could request something, we'd fill the order from inventory on the shelf, and the customer would have it a lot sooner."

"Folks are impatient these days, that's for sure. Those big internet companies guarantee two-day shipping if you pay for it."

"Exactly. Of course, your products would all still be handmade, but quicker service will give you an edge over other home decor retailers."

When she paused for breath, Brian realized that she must have rehearsed this little spiel before presenting her idea to him. It was another example of how much the impulsive girl he'd known had matured into an intelligent, thoughtful woman. Much as he liked the difference, he found himself hoping that once her life calmed down a bit, that girl might poke her head out again.

He kind of missed her. She was a lot of fun.

Appalled by his errant train of thought, he firmly brought his head back to the matter at hand. "Jordan's the artist, but I can make pretty much anything if it's not real fancy. What'd you have in mind?"

In reply, she swiveled the monitor so he could see the screen. Apparently, she'd been researching various online vendors that offered iron products ranging from napkin holders to mug trees. "This could work. These things are small, and I could probably knock together several in a good day."

"I like these," she said excitedly, flipping to another screen to show him a selection of wall-mounted sayings. "They're a single word, and then you can put them together to make your own phrase."

"The cutout ones are cool, too. I've seen guys on TV using lasers to make stuff like that."

"Lasers?" she teased. "Don't you think that's a little out of place in a shop that keeps a coal fire burning from one day to the next?"

"Good point. Maybe we can add that later." Tilting her head, she gave him a look he couldn't begin to identify. "What?"

"You said 'we,'" she commented in a soft, vulnerable voice that reminded him just how far she'd fallen. "Does that mean you think of us as a team?"

Did he? When she first showed up on his doorstep, he never would've considered it. But there was no denying that Lindsay had the skills he was sorely lacking, and her take-charge attitude had freed him from some of the worry that had been weighing him down. He'd been concerned about feeling more pressure because of his obligation to Lindsay and her baby.

In truth, he felt less. Maybe because while he'd taken on some of Lindsay's burden, in return she'd accepted some of his. That was the way his parents had always been, sharing the tough times, celebrating the good ones. Their partnership was more than a marriage, and he'd long ago realized that was why he was still single.

The easy part was finding a woman to love, who loved him in return. He'd had a few long-term relationships, and for one reason or another, they hadn't lasted. The hard part—the one he hadn't mastered yet—was feeling that kind of devotion for someone who matched him on some deeper level. Someone who found a way to reach the piece of him that he normally kept to himself.

When it occurred to him that Lindsay was still waiting for him to respond, he opted for humor. "Well, two people don't make much of a team."

"That depends on the people, doesn't it?"

"Yeah, I guess it does."

That got him a delighted smile, and as she shifted her attention back to their list, he grinned despite himself.

"Lindsay?" When she glanced up, he said, "I wanna thank you for everything you've done. Things would be a lot bleaker without you. At the forge, I mean," he added quickly, just to make sure he was being clear.

"You're very welcome. I should thank you for taking a chance on me. Not many people would have, under the circumstances."

Crossing his arms on the desk, he leaned forward to show her he meant what he was about to say. "Can I make a suggestion?"

"You're the boss."

She held her fingers over the keys as if preparing to take more notes, and he shook his head. "I mean, as me."

"Oh." Resting her hands in her lap, she gave him a curious look. "Go ahead."

"How 'bout if we both agree to let the past be in the past, and go on from here? That way, you can stop apologizing for what happened years ago."

"Does that mean you forgive me?"

Until recently, Brian never would've thought that kind of thing was possible. But now, sitting here with the woman who'd singlehandedly helped him save his fledgling business, he couldn't imagine anything else. Smiling, he said, "Yes, Lindsay, I forgive you."

She beamed at him as if he'd just granted her fondest wish. "If I could get out of this chair gracefully, I'd hug you."

"No problem. I'll settle for that smile."

"Really?"

"Sure. I always loved seeing you happy."

He hadn't intended to say that out loud, but when those incredible blue eyes brightened with joy, he decided maybe it hadn't been such a bad idea, after all.

"You know," she said, giving him a decidedly feminine smirk, "for an arrogant jock, you're really sweet."

He recognized the backhanded compliment from their high school days, and he came back with, "And for a brainiac, you're an awesome cheerleader."

They both burst out laughing, and she put a hand on her stomach. "The baby's dancing around in there."

"She must like it when you laugh."

"Do you want to feel?"

"Seriously?" She nodded, and then guided his palm to the right spot. He felt a wriggling movement, and met her eyes in disbelief. "That's incredible."

"I know. Sometimes it still amazes me that there's a little person in there, moving around, growing, getting ready to be born. It makes me want to be the best mom ever, even when I'm not sure what that means."

"You'll figure it out," Brian assured her as he sat back. "Mom and Gran will be around, so you won't have to do everything by yourself."

"And now I have a job, so things are looking up for us."

Her upbeat tone sounded a bit forced to him, but he knew there was nothing more he could do. So, because he was a practical sort of guy, he settled on logic. "If we're gonna keep moving in that direction, we'd better get back to work on this website."

"As soon as I use the bathroom."

Brian chuckled, but didn't say anything as he helped her to her feet and then stacked her sketches for future reference. For the next six weeks, he'd be getting a first-hand education in how to deal with a pregnant woman.

He had a feeling that before winter was over, things were going to get a lot more interesting.

Chapter Seven

"Emma, these are fabulous!"

Across Ellie's dining room table were spread a dozen posters of varying sizes, with all manner of hearts and ribbons curling around elegant calligraphy of details for the upcoming Sweetheart Dance. Brian had been dead-on in his prediction: Lindsay had been unanimously voted in as chairwoman and now had her hands fuller than ever. With Valentine's Day a scant two weeks away, she'd gone into what her new boss called her "major general" mode and put out the call for help from wherever she could get it.

The first person to respond had been Emma Calhoun.

Lindsay remembered her as a pixie-ish girl who harassed her older brothers every chance she got. Today, she was dressed in soft winter layers and a pale blue woolen hat, looking as adorable as a cancer patient could possibly be. How she held up so well under the rigors of chemo amazed Lindsay, who vowed then and there to stop complaining about her swollen ankles.

"Thanks," the young woman beamed, a bit of color

pinking her pale cheeks. "I love doing the kids' projects with them at school, but it's fun to design something for grown-ups."

"Well, these are exactly what I had in mind," Lindsay complimented her, shuffling through the posters to the large banner underneath. "We just started working on the dance last week. How did you get all these done so fast?"

Glancing around, Emma leaned in as if she was sharing a huge secret. "I had my middle-schoolers help me. The boys weren't into it, but the girls jumped right in."

"That explains all the glitter," Lindsay commented with a chuckle. Then an idea popped into her head, and she said, "I know parents are probably looking forward to an adult evening, but do you think we should do something for kids, too? Parents could drop them off, come to the dance, then pick them up afterward, like you did for New Year's Eve."

Emma's china blue eyes lit up with genuine enthusiasm. "That's a great idea! You're really starting to think like a mom."

Lindsay wasn't sure about that, but she didn't want to sound ungracious, so she smiled. "Thanks."

"Are you scared?" Emma asked. "I apologize if that's out of line, but if it was me, I'd be terrified."

"With what you're going through? I doubt it."

"But that only involves me," she explained, holding out her arms to emphasize her point. "What you're doing is so much more intimidating, because you're doing it for someone else."

No one had ever expressed it to her that way, and Lindsay rolled the concept around in her mind before realizing that Emma had nailed her emotions on the head. "I guess you're right. I haven't been able to pin down why I felt that way until now, though."

"I don't know about you, but I like having an idea of what I'm up against. Then I can decide how to attack it and beat it into the ground."

Gritty and full of determination, the statement was a glimpse into the character of the woman who was fighting such a horrible disease with everything she had. If Emma was able keep her spirits up during cancer treatments, Lindsay realized there was hope for her, too. "How do you stay so upbeat?"

"It's not easy sometimes," she admitted quietly. "When things get tough, you need a little faith to fall back on."

"It's nice to have that."

"Yeah, it is. And having family around you doesn't hurt, either," Emma added, smiling at someone behind Lindsay.

When she turned, she found Brian standing in the open archway, hands in the pockets of his heavy-duty jean jacket. "Yeah, yeah, yeah. Why'm I getting the feeling I'm about to get roped into something?"

"We need help hanging these posters around town," Lindsay informed him coolly. "And you're taller than both of us."

"Combined," Emma added with a giggle.

"So I'm better than a ladder?"

"Mostly," Lindsay allowed, giving him a little smirk. "Plus you're more entertaining."

"Mostly," Emma echoed, and the two of them broke up laughing. Brian didn't look thrilled, and his sister quickly went over to him, going up on tiptoe to kiss his cheek. "We're just teasing, big brother. We do actually need some help with these, if you have time."

"You know I do." The adoring smile he gave her told Lindsay just how much he cherished his little sister. "You're acting like you feel good today."

"I do." He gave her a skeptical once-over, and she laughed. "Honest. Don't be so gloomy. The treatments are done now, and my hair's coming back nicely. I'll be back to my old self in time for summer vacation."

"I'm counting on it." Doubt clouded Brian's eyes, but to his credit, he masked it with a smile that was very convincing but didn't fool anyone.

"Well, I have some errands to run," Emma said, zipping up her cute lavender ski jacket, "so I should get going. I'll be back in time for the committee meeting."

"Thanks again," Lindsay said, giving the fragile-looking art teacher a gentle hug. "And please let your students know they did a first-rate job."

"I will. They'll be really excited to hear there's going to be a party for them, too."

After she'd gone, Brian gave Lindsay an accusing look. "There's gonna be a what?"

Lindsay outlined her kernel of an idea, and he nodded. "Sounds like fun. But you're not gonna trick me to play ringleader for that, are you?"

"Not unless you want to."

"Actually," he said, strolling into the dining room, "I was thinking I'd go to the dance."

They hadn't discussed anything beyond logistics for making the event happen, so his revelation caught Lindsay off guard. "Oh, sure." Realizing that sounded lame, she tried again. "I mean, you should do what you want."

"Would you mind if I asked someone?"

"Of course not," she replied, a little more forcefully than she'd intended. Smoothing out her tone, she dredged up a smile. "Why would I mind?"

As he stared down at her, one of those infernal grins quirked the corner of his mouth. "'Cause I was thinking of asking you."

"You were not," she sputtered, backpedaling to put some space between them. The grin was widening, and she crossed her arms defensively. "You're yanking my chain, aren't you?"

The grin evaporated instantly, and he shook his head with a somber expression. "Never."

"Look at me," she pressed, opening her arms to give him a clear view. "I'm hardly dating material these days."

In truth, she suspected that her carefree dating time was probably over for good. Her own mother had blithely skipped from man to man, peppering Lindsay's childhood with one sketchy father figure after another. There was no way she'd do that to her own child, so there wouldn't be any just-for-fun guys in her life anymore. She needed a steady, solid man who would stand beside her through good times and bad. And if Jeff had taught her anything, it was that trustworthy men were becoming exceedingly hard to find.

"So it won't be a date," Brian suggested easily, as if it wasn't that big of a deal. "We'll just be two friendly coworkers spending Valentine's Day at a charity dance to help rebuild the bridge. No strings, just doing our part for a good cause."

Brian had always had a knack for making her believe that everything would be fine, even when that seemed impossible to her. Lindsay recognized that she had a pessimistic streak, and circumstances had hardened it into a gloomy view of the world that she'd love to escape. She just didn't know how.

But here he was, offering her a respite from the incessant worry that dominated her thoughts and tripped her up when she least expected it. He made them going to the dance as friends sound plausible—and possibly even entertaining. She had to admit it would be nice to spend an evening with a man who didn't have designs on getting anything from her beyond a few dances.

"Okay," she finally agreed. "It would be nice to have some fun for a change."

"My thoughts exactly. We've both been working like mules, and I think we've earned a night out."

It was sweet of him to be so concerned about her, she thought with a smile. She couldn't have invented a better boss if she'd tried. Someone knocked on the front door, and she heard Ellie greeting their first arrivals. "Absolutely. But for now, we have that meeting. Will you second my motion for the kids' party?"

"Absolutely," he repeated, grinning.

"Thanks."

"For the invite or the backup?"

"Both. It's been a long time since I had someone in my life that I could count on."

Tears welled in her eyes, and she blinked hard to keep them at bay. She hadn't meant to say that last part out loud, and she cringed at the weakness she heard in her voice. To his credit, Brian never hesitated.

Taking her into his arms, he held her close enough that she could feel his heart beating against her cheek. Burrowing into the quiet strength he offered, she relished the unfamiliar feeling of being protected from whatever the world might decide to throw at her.

"I'll never let you down, Lindsay. You have my word on that."

And because it was Brian, she believed him.

After all these years, Lindsay Holland still had the power to amaze him.

Brian sat midway down one side of Gran's large kitchen table, munching his way through a piece of cinnamon swirl coffee cake so tender he hardly had to chew it. He kept a casual expression plastered on his face, even while he marveled at Lindsay's ability to be in tears one minute and completely composed the next. If he hadn't seen it for himself, he never would've believed she'd been so distraught earlier.

No doubt about it: the woman had backbone.

Gran caught his eye, giving him a curious look that clearly said she knew something wasn't quite right with him. He deflected the concern with a grin, and though she didn't seem convinced, she refocused her attention on the discussion about the silent auction prizes that had already been donated.

"Ten free car washes," Lindsay was saying, "free tree trimming in the spring and four hours of handyman services from Sam Calhoun." Pausing, she smiled at Holly. "That should be very popular and bring in a ton of money. Be sure to thank him for us."

"Will do," Holly agreed, returning the smile. "Now if I can just get him to actually come to the dance, it will be a good Valentine's Day."

The women around the table laughed in unison, and Brian chuckled at the comment. His reserved big brother wasn't much for socializing, but he'd been attending a lot more town events lately. Brian had a feeling it was more to make his wife happy than from an actual desire to join in, but it was still good to see them out together.

Thoughts of being out together made him wonder how folks would react when they saw him at the dance with Lindsay. Their tumultuous relationship might be in the past, but he knew that in a small town like Liberty Creek, their unexpected reunion was big news. Especially in the middle of a long winter when folks had cabin fever and were eager for anything to break up the tedium. Even though he and Lindsay were keeping things on a just-friends level, he had no doubt that some people would assume otherwise.

He also had no doubt that Lindsay would set them straight. She'd made it clear that she wasn't ready for any emotional entanglements, which suited him perfectly. At least, that's what he kept telling himself. Then there were more personal moments like her minibreakdown, when she'd turned to him for comfort and he'd stepped up just like he used to. Because he simply couldn't help himself.

Either he was a complete moron, he mused as he snagged another piece of cake, or his feelings for her weren't as far in the past as he wanted to believe. Then again, he was exhausted beyond anything he'd ever experienced before resurrecting his family's old business. He wasn't used to dealing with that level of stress, and he reasoned that it probably had a lot to do with why he was feeling this way.

Once the forge started consistently bringing in some cash, he'd feel better.

"And that brings me to something new I'd like to propose," Lindsay was saying, her urgent look dragging

Brian back from his mental stroll. She quickly outlined the concept of hosting a kids' party the same night.

The idea prompted an instant buzz, with suggestions for refreshments and activities from face painting to kid-friendly movies. When it died down, she made the motion official. Brian took his cue and raised his hand to second it. The "yes" vote was unanimous, and the delight on Lindsay's face was unmistakable. Knowing how isolated she sometimes felt, he understood how important it was to her that she not only be involved in the fund-raising project, but also do the best job she could.

"That's wonderful," she approved, jotting a note on her lined pad. "I'll be putting together an email blast to reach families around the area who are active online. But there's nothing like good, old-fashioned word of mouth to get people excited about something. I'm hoping you can all help with that."

Brian thought it was interesting that the shiny new laptop was nowhere to be seen. Then he recalled her comment about technology intimidating some people, and he suspected that was why she'd gone old-school for this meeting. Folks in Liberty Creek weren't necessarily against progress, but they were traditional, and they liked to keep things simple.

After a few more items, she read through the list of assignments and reminded everyone that their next meeting was in a week.

"I know everyone's busy, but we need to keep up the pace," she reminded them in a bright, upbeat tone, adding a smile for good measure. "The bridge work is vital to everyone in Liberty Creek who relies on tourist trade during the good weather."

"That'd be everyone in Liberty Creek," Hal Rogers

echoed her comment, getting nods of agreement from around the table. "I'll be taking one of those posters with me, that's for sure. I get a lot of traffic in the barbershop this time of year."

Lindsay thanked him and then the entire group for giving up their evening to help out. On their way to the door, several people took posters from the stack, and before long the dining room table was clear of all but the largest one.

Folding her arms in obvious displeasure, Lindsay scowled. "It's so pretty. I hate to see it sitting here instead of being displayed out in the open somewhere."

"Brian can put it up in the bakery," Gran suggested while she pushed one of the armchairs back into place. Then she gave him "The Look."

"Can't you, honey?" she prodded.

"Yes, ma'am," he agreed without hesitation. To his knowledge, no one ever said no to Ellie Calhoun, and he wasn't about to tempt fate by being the first. "I'll pick it up in the morning and get it hung before your assistant manager opens for breakfast."

"That wasn't so hard, was it?" Gran crowed, catching Lindsay around the shoulders for a quick embrace. "Most problems have a solution, if you just know where to look."

Brian chuckled. "I just can't figure out why you're always looking at me."

"Because you're tall and good with a hammer?" Lindsay asked, blue eyes twinkling with the kind of humor he was noticing more often lately. It was encouraging to see some of her old spark coming back, even briefly.

A quick circuit with the trash can cleared the kitchen table, and before he knew it, the house was back to normal. "Okay, then. Do you ladies need anything before I head out?"

"No, honey," Gran told him, walking him to the door the way she always did. "Go home and get some sleep."

"Thanks for everything," Lindsay added, rewarding him with a smile warmed by gratitude. "I know meetings aren't your thing, but you were great tonight."

"Just following orders, boss."

That earned him the laugh he'd been after, and she opened the door for him. "I'm looking forward to you being the boss tomorrow. It's not easy being the one in charge."

"Tell me about it."

He stepped out, and she shut the door behind him. A couple inches of snow had fallen, coating the brick steps and walkway enough that he shoveled and salted them before he left for home.

Since it wasn't all that cold, he took his time strolling along the sidewalk, admiring the still beauty of a crisp winter's night. There wasn't a single cloud in the sky, and the stars overhead glittered like gems in a jeweler's display. The waxing moon hung low over the trees, its light reflecting off the snow and bathing the town in a hazy glow.

Since moving back to his hometown, this was the first time that he'd slowed down enough to really appreciate his surroundings. The charming houses, the trees covered in snow, the gazebo strung with tiny white lights for no reason other than because it was pretty that way. Portsmouth might have had more nightlife and restaurants, but to be honest, he didn't miss them all that much. Been there, done that, he figured with a mental shrug.

In his heart, he guessed that he was still a small-town boy. And now that he was back, he couldn't remember why he'd been in such a hurry to leave.

While he was mulling that over, he turned the corner and headed up the short path that led to the dark cottage. To his surprise, there was something on his small porch. He'd forgotten to leave the carriage lights on— again—so he turned on his phone's flashlight and went up the snowy steps to see what was in front of his door.

A dog.

Curled up on the welcome mat Emma had gotten him as a housewarming gift, seemingly sound asleep. Its shaggy, matted fur was every color he'd ever seen on an animal, and even in the narrow beam of light it was obvious that the poor creature had dropped here in an exhausted heap.

"Hey, there," he said softly, to avoid startling the mutt. He wasn't keen on being attacked by a frightened animal that might tear his legs to pieces before he could get it under control.

Nothing.

A horrible thought entered his mind, and he knelt on the sagging floorboards for a closer look. The patchy fur rose and fell with each breath, and he was relieved to know the dog was alive. There was no collar, and he didn't recognize it as belonging to anyone he knew. A quick glance around showed him that no one was out hunting for a lost pet.

He reached out a tentative hand, ready to yank it back at the first sign of aggression. When he gently stroked its forehead, the dog slowly opened its eyes. And then, to his astonishment, it let out a shuddering whimper and gave him the most pathetic look he'd seen in his life.

"Aw, man," Brian muttered, rubbing his neck while he considered what to do. Everyone knew that letting a stray dog into the house was the first step on the road to being its new owner. But it was below freezing now, and the forecast was predicting single digits by morning. He wasn't exactly looking for a furry roommate, but he couldn't just leave this lost mongrel outside on a night like this. Or any other, for that matter.

"Okay," he finally said, getting to his feet to unlock the door. "But just for tonight."

The dog rolled over but stayed in its prone position, gazing curiously into the dark house. Brian thought maybe it didn't want to risk venturing into unfamiliar territory that it couldn't see, so he reached around the door frame to snap on the living room lights. Now those ears were twitching, and his canine visitor looked up at him, angling its head in a questioning pose.

Stepping inside, Brian held the door open. "Come on in."

Letting out a quick yip of thanks, the dog trotted inside and sat politely in front of him. Another yip, and this time it offered a mangy paw in a very humanlike greeting that made Brian laugh.

"Nice to meet you." A quick assessment showed him that his guest was male—and even filthier than he'd originally realized. "Okay, here's the plan. We're gonna scarf up some dinner for you, then it's straight into the tub. Got it?"

That got him two excited barks, and his new buddy went up on his back paws, wrapping the front ones around Brian's waist. The show of canine gratitude was rewarding, and Brian had to admit that once you got past the dog's rough condition, he was pretty cute.

Alarmed by the direction his thoughts had taken, he paused in front of the fridge and pointed down at the excited pup. "Let's get one thing straight, dude. You're not staying. Understood?"

The dog yipped, cocking his head again in what seemed to be a habit for him. Trying not to be impressed, Brian filled a bowl with cold water to keep the dog occupied while he nuked some leftover beef stew in the microwave.

The stray scarfed down what had probably been his best meal in weeks, and when he looked up, Brian noticed that the crazy markings extended to his eyes, which were a crystalline blue with silvery starbursts surrounding the pupils. Definitely unusual, he mused, and something he should add to the lost-dog flyers he'd be putting up around town tomorrow morning.

When the bowls were empty, he clapped his hands to get the mutt's attention. "Okay, dude, it's bath time. I sure hope you don't hate water."

The dog trotted at his heels as if he was on an invisible leash, which was a sure sign he'd been someone's pet at one point. Judging by his bedraggled condition, that had been a while ago. On the way to the bathroom, it occurred to him that a wet dog might catch a chill on a night like this, so he paused to start a fire that would warm the air.

Thankfully, his mysterious houseguest was as well behaved in the tub as he'd been everywhere else, and by the time he was rinsed, it was obvious just how lean the poor guy had gotten while he'd been on his own. Brian couldn't imagine why anyone would leave such a great dog to fend for himself, and his temper began boiling when he considered what kind of person would toss a sweet-tempered creature like this out into the snow.

"Well, you're here now, warm and safe." His canine visitor circled a few times in front of the hearth, then sank down on the floor and let out an enormous yawn. It struck him as a very human thing to do, and Brian laughed. "Yeah, I know how you feel. Guess it's bedtime for both of us."

Patting the furry forehead, he went into his bedroom and closed the door behind him. He hadn't even climbed into bed when he heard a quiet whimper on the other side. He ignored it, assuming the dog would get sick of it and stop. Instead, the whimpering got louder, and then it was joined by a soft scratching on the thick wooden jamb.

After all the poor guy had been through, Brian didn't have the heart to leave him alone in the front room. So, because he was a softy, he grabbed his pillow and one of his mother's quilts and opened the door. Silhouetted in the open frame sat his new pal, swishing his feathery tail over the floorboards with a hopeful expression.

"Okay, you got me. I'm a sucker for big blue eyes." The tail swishing quickened, and as Brian trudged back into the living room, the dog danced around him in obvious delight. Chuckling to himself, Brian stretched out on the sofa and got comfortable. Glancing over, he caught the expectant look in the stray's eyes and grumbled, "What?"

A tentative paw sneaked onto the cushion in front of him, and he laughed. "Seriously?"

That got him a definitive yip, which he took for a yes. So he wedged himself to the back of the couch and patted the quilt in invitation. He didn't have to do it twice.

Once they were both jammed into place, his damp visitor curled into a ball, resting his head on his paws with a weary sigh. And, despite the odd detour his night had taken, Brian drifted off with a smile on his face.

Chapter Eight

When Lindsay arrived at work the next day, she got quite the surprise.

"Well, hello there," she greeted the dog sitting beside the desk while Brian continued his running battle with the computer. Hanging her coat on its hook, she said, "You didn't mention hiring anyone new."

Glancing up from the screen, Brian chuckled. "He was on my porch when I got home last night. No collar or anything, but someone trained him well, so I'm gonna hang up some flyers and hopefully find his owner. As soon as I figure out how to make them, that is."

"Good idea." The pup offered her a paw, and she shook it gently. "Nice to meet you."

"I tried to get him to stay in the house, but he wouldn't stop barking so I caved and brought him with me."

"You have a new tagalong. That's so cute."

"Whatever."

"Oh, please," she scoffed, laughing off the obvious attempt at bravado. "You love dogs, and I'd imagine you won't be too disappointed if no one claims this one."

"Well, maybe not," he allowed, leaning back in the

chair with a grin that reminded her there was still a little boy inside that tall, rangy frame.

"What's his name?"

"Haven't thought of one, since I'm not sure he'll be sticking around."

Lindsay studied the fur ball and said, "It's obvious that he hasn't been getting fed, so he's either lost or someone left him behind when they moved. My guess is he's yours if you want him."

"I'm no good at thinking up names. I've been calling him 'dude.'"

"Very original." After a moment, she said, "How about Riley?"

Brian looked down and asked, "Whatta you think, boy?" The dog immediately responded by tipping his head back and letting out an enthusiastic little yip. "Sounds like a winner to me, too. We'll go with that."

"Good enough. Would you like me to save you from designing that lost-dog flyer?"

"Please."

They both laughed, and Lindsay shooed Brian out so she could get to work. After his story about Riley trailing after him everywhere, she expected the stray to follow him into the shop. Instead, he crawled under the desk and stretched out, pillowing his head on Lindsay's shoes. It was an unusual way to work, but once she got used to it, he wasn't a distraction, and she had to admit that he made an excellent foot warmer.

When Brian came back in around lunchtime, she had another surprise for him. Handing over a printed page, she tried to look casual as he took in what it said.

Meeting her eyes over the top of the paper, he asked, "Is this what I think it is?"

"That depends on what you think it is."

"Our first order from outside the area. From Marion Granger in Framingham, Massachusetts."

"Then it's what you think," she confirmed, touched by the way he'd referred to the momentous occurrence as "our" order. Slipping her feet out from underneath her sleeping assistant, she went around the desk to hug him. "Congratulations, Brian. You're on your way."

"Thanks." He stared down at the paper again as if he still couldn't quite believe it was real. When his eyes met hers again, they warmed as he smiled. "It wouldn't have happened without the website you designed to bring in new customers."

His praise settled nicely over her still-recovering ego, which made it easy to be gracious. "Your work sells itself. I told you that once you showed people what you can do, they'd be lining up to buy things from Liberty Creek Forge."

"Lining up?"

Laughing, Lindsay reached into the wire basket on her desk labeled Orders to Fill. Feeling almost giddy, she handed him a dozen more printouts, each one requesting a different item from the stock he'd been working so hard to build. As if that weren't enough, there was one from a couple in Florida requesting a quote for a custom garden trellis that would serve as the focal point of their daughter's upcoming wedding.

"Whoa," he breathed, sounding a little overwhelmed. "Looks like I'm gonna be busy."

"And successful. Just like I always knew you would be."

The last part jumped out all on its own, and she felt her cheeks heating with embarrassment. This was a professional achievement for him, and she hadn't intended to make it personal in any way. But when she saw the grateful look in his eyes, she was glad she'd said it.

"You did?"

"Sure," she responded, hunting for a way to make it sound less intimate. Then it hit her, and she nonchalantly added, "Everyone did. I mean, that's why your class voted you 'most likely to succeed' your senior year."

"That's right, they did," he commented with a chuckle. "A lot of them still live around here. I wonder what they think of me now."

"I can't speak for everyone, but I'm pretty impressed."

That got her one of those lazy grins that still had a way of making her wary heart roll over in her chest. Brian Calhoun had always been hard to resist, but she had more than herself to think about, and she knew that she had to be less impulsive. Over the years, her reckless heart had gotten her into more trouble than she preferred to think about. Right now, getting romantically involved with anyone—especially the man who signed her paychecks—was the most foolish thing she could do.

Fortunately, someone knocking on the front door broke the moment, and they both looked toward the sound. A tall man in a black dress coat stood outside the glass, and he raised a gloved hand in greeting.

"Were you expecting company?" Brian asked as he went to unlock the door.

"No."

"Can't imagine anyone coming up to this end of town on such a cold day by mistake." Clearly baffled, he opened the door and stepped back to let the man inside. "Can I help you?"

"Good morning," the stranger replied, pulling off his leather driving gloves in a practiced motion. Offering his hand, he said, "I'm Rick Marshall, the commercial loan officer at the new Patriot's Bank branch here in Liberty Creek. Now that Fred Gilbert has retired, I'm responsible for overseeing your account."

Brian took the man's business card and said, "I'm Brian Calhoun, the guy who signed all those papers last fall. It's nice to meet you. Have you heard how Fred and Dillie are enjoying Florida?"

"No, but it wouldn't surprise me if they're patting themselves on the back right about now." Rick glanced out the window and grimaced. "They picked a good year to go."

"Aw, this is nothin'," Brian assured him with a grin. "Couple years ago, we were socked in from Christmas straight through to Mother's Day."

A look of horror crossed the poor man's face. "You're kidding."

"Yes, he is," Lindsay assured him, coming forward to rescue him from a full-on Calhoun ribbing session. Holding out her hand, she introduced herself.

Feeling genuine sympathy for him, she gave him her friendliest smile. She'd gotten adept at dealing with financial types during her legal assistant career, and she'd quickly learned that a little extra attention went a long way. "Come on in and have some coffee and a muffin. That should help thaw you out."

"Muffin?" he echoed as he followed them into the office. "From the bakery here in town?"

"The same," Brian told him as he filled one of the

beefy Liberty Creek Forge mugs and handed it over. "Ellie Calhoun's the best baker in the state. Not to mention my grandmother."

"I've taken my daughters in there a couple times. Your grandmother has a real way with kids."

Brian chuckled. "She's had a lotta practice."

Lindsay cleared a space for the three of them to sit and made small talk while they enjoyed their snack. Frequent glimpses of Brian's expression showed her that while he appeared to be calm enough, the wheels in his head were spinning as quickly as ever. No doubt he was trying to figure out why on earth a bank officer had come by on the coldest morning of the winter.

From her bookkeeping work, she knew that the business loan he'd taken out for the forge was a substantial one, and although he made every payment on time, it was by the skin of his teeth. She was pondering other possibilities for the visit when she heard a rumbling noise coming from under the desk.

Rick stopped midsentence and gave Brian a questioning look.

"Sorry, just our shop mascot. Come here, Riley, and say hello."

Since they really had no idea what the dog's name was, Lindsay was amazed when he obeyed Brian's command without so much as a whimper. Trotting over, he sat in front of Rick and held out his paw in welcome.

"Hello to you, too," the banker responded, chuckling as they shook. After a long look, he asked, "I've never seen a dog with those markings before. What breed is he?"

"An Australian shepherd," Lindsay replied quickly, hoping to save Brian the embarrassment of having to admit he had no clue about the dog's pedigree. He gave her a curious glance, and she explained. "I looked it up online."

"Huh. So computers are good for something other than torturing me?"

"I feel the same way about them." Laughing, Rick set his empty mug on the table. "My girls would love a dog. Now that we're living here and have a fenced yard, it'd be nice to have one. In the spring I'll have to look around for a good kennel."

Lindsay got the distinct impression that his friendly manner was aimed at putting them at ease, and in her experience that usually wasn't a good sign. She decided it would be smart to cut to the chase and find out what he wanted. "Is there something we can do for you, Rick? I just closed the books for January if you're interested in doing a quick audit."

"She's good," he commented to Brian, then sat back with what sounded like a genuine sigh of regret. "I hate dancing around, so I won't sugarcoat it for you. It's come to our attention that Fred approved your loan based in part on his long-standing relationship with your family. While we don't question your intent to repay the loan, we are concerned about the more practical aspects of the arrangement. Our main branch in Waterford sent me to assess how viable this business is given the current economic climate in the area."

Lindsay's heart sank. This was Brian's greatest fear, that the ironworks would fail before it even got started. The orders that had come in recently were a good start, but she knew they were far from enough to convince a business-minded man like Rick Marshall that the newly resurrected forge was a good risk for his bank to take.

To her astonishment, Brian laughed. "Drew the short straw, huh?"

"Yes," Rick admitted on a heavy exhale. "Actually, I have a suspicion that all the straws were short, and this is my hazing."

The two of them laughed, and it occurred to her that Brian's easygoing personality had turned what could have been an awkward encounter into the first step in the men becoming friends.

Brian stood and opened the office door. "How 'bout I give you a tour, then show you what I'm working on right now? Then if you've got questions about anything I'm doing here, we'll talk."

"That'd be great. I'd love to see how a vintage blacksmith shop operates."

The line was straight out of the marketing section of their new website, and as Lindsay watched them go, she had to admit that she was impressed.

Now, if only Brian could charm Rick Marshall the way he did everyone else he met, they'd still be in business. If not...

Pushing the thought aside, she settled in her spot behind the desk and opened her accounting program. When a local bank expressed doubts about continuing to fund a business just up the street, that was a serious red flag. She might not be a craftsman, but a slew of professional-looking reports could ease the loan committee's concerns about Liberty Creek Forge. Brian was paying her to run this end of his business, after all. As with the intimidating stack of environmental documentation she'd completed, this was a chance for her to prove to him just how valuable she could be.

When he popped his head back into the office and

said her name, she all but jumped out of her chair. "Don't sneak up on people like that! You scared me half to death."

"Sorry. I was wondering if you've got a few minutes to help me show Rick around the place."

Having resigned herself to being relegated to the office, she was flattered that he'd even think of asking. "Well, sure, but why?"

"You're the one who set up the showroom to be photographed for the website, and I thought it'd be better for him to hear the strategy from you."

There was something else at play here, and Lindsay quickly figured it out. "Since you weren't listening when I explained it to you."

"Basically." She tilted her head in a chiding gesture, and he laughed. "Okay, you got me. Can you bail me out one more time? I want him to think I actually know what I'm doing here, and I figure showing him that I hire smart people is a solid place to start."

"Trying to get on my good side?" she asked around a laugh that bubbled up on its own.

As she joined him at the door, he flashed her one of those shameless Calhoun grins. "Always. It's way safer than your bad side."

"And don't you forget it."

She hadn't felt this feisty in a long time, and it occurred to her that her confidence, which had been on a steady decline for months, had rebounded without her even noticing. Brian had a lot to do with that, and as she approached the visiting banker, she vowed to find a way to repay him for his faith in her.

Brian had built the small but well-lit display area from seasoned planks he'd found stashed in the old building's rafters, and Lindsay thought the room had a rustic charm that suited his products perfectly. There were candlesticks, napkin holders, towel bars and even a couple of hanging pot racks. As Rick inspected them, he nodded a few times, which Lindsay interpreted as approval.

Then he turned with a smile. "These are really nice, and each one is a little different from the others. I've never seen anything like them."

"Everything's made by these," Brian explained, holding up his callused hands. A little glimmer came into his eyes, and he asked, "Would you like a demonstration?"

"Would I— Absolutely!" the loan officer replied with enthusiasm that had to be for real. Because of his stylish clothes and Italian shoes, she hadn't pegged him for a craft lover. Apparently she'd misread him completely.

Brian had to refire the banked coals, but that gave him the chance to show Rick how the archaic operation worked. After engaging the all-important air scrubber, he stirred up the embers and tossed in several shovelfuls of coal. Grasping the thick wooden handle of the restored bellows, he leveraged his considerable strength into the job of whipping up the flames before adding more coal.

The fire crackled in response, and he slid in a slender rod of metal. "We got an order for a trivet yesterday. The client wants it to be in the shape of a Celtic knot, so eventually there will be a lot of pieces welded in. But it starts like this."

Before long, the iron was red-hot, and he pulled it from the fire. Resting it on an anvil the founders of the ironworks had hauled from Pennsylvania to New Hampshire in one of their wagons, he chose a meaty-looking hammer from a nearby rack of tools.

"It needs to be round," he explained in between ringing whacks, "so I keep turning and hitting, heating it up when it starts to cool too much to shape."

Then, like the showman he was, he dunked the evolving rod in a bucket of water, unleashing a cloud of hissing steam that served as the ideal punctuation mark to his running commentary. While he worked, Lindsay couldn't help feeling as if she was witnessing history right before her eyes. If you ignored the faded jeans and rock concert T-shirt, Brian could have easily been at home in a blacksmith shop from a hundred years ago. She knew what he made, of course, but she'd been so occupied with running the business that she hadn't gotten the chance to watch him actually make the products she was trying to market.

It was impressive, to say the least.

Judging by his awed expression, Rick Marshall thought so, too.

"This is amazing," he said, stepping in for a closer look at the sturdy tools of the Calhoun family trade. Glancing around, he went on, "Is this all original equipment?"

"Mostly. The air scrubber's modern, and my brother Sam helped me get the electrical and plumbing up to code. Other than that, it's pretty much the way it was the day Jeremiah Calhoun and his brothers opened the place in 1820."

"Your website mentions that you'll be offering live demonstrations in the spring. Doing this for one person is a lot different from hosting groups of tourists. Do you really think that timetable is realistic?"

Brian grinned away the skepticism. "Probably not, but we'll make it work. We always do," he added, including Lindsay in the conversation with a smile that filled her with pride. It was so sweet of him to do that, she felt obligated to back him up.

"The school used to send students here for a living history lesson with Brian's grandfather," she explained. "We've already got a visit booked for early May, and other classes are just waiting for a good time to come in."

"They're in for a real treat, that's for sure." After another look around, Rick said, "Okay, you've convinced me. You've been making your payments right along, which works in your favor because it's tough for a new business to get up and running. Taking advantage of the tourist season is a great wrinkle, and now that I've met you and Lindsay, I'm confident you'll make good use of the money. I can't promise anything on my own, but my recommendation should give you a boost with the board when they do their review."

"And that will reassure them that Fred's approval was based on the numbers rather than a personal bias," Lindsay suggested.

"Let's hope so. I'm going to recommend foregoing the balloon payment and allowing the loan to continue on a standard payment schedule. That will give you to the end of the summer to pay everything off. I'll let you know as soon as I have an official ruling from the loan committee."

He offered his hand, and Brian held up his filthy palms in warning. Chuckling, Rick kept his own hand in place and they shook to seal their new arrangement. Rick stopped in the office to pick up the reports Lindsay had printed for him. After giving Riley a pat on the head, he said goodbye and left.

Brian's chiseled features were set in a pensive look, and she wondered what was going on in that agile mind of his. She waited for him to share, but grew impatient when he didn't say anything. "What?"

"I'm thinking somebody asked him to come by and check out the forge in person."

"That makes sense, but who?" He raised an eyebrow at her, and she laughed. "Ellie. That would be just like her, wouldn't it?"

"He said he and his daughters have been to the bakery. You know how Gran loves to mingle with her customers, find out all about them. In a couple minutes, she would've known more about Rick than other folks would learn in a month."

"And he wouldn't even realize what was happening," Lindsay added with a grin. "She does have a way with people."

"Yeah, she does."

His tone wasn't amused anymore, and Lindsay frowned at the somber direction his mood had taken. "Don't let that upset you, Brian. She might have sent Rick here, but it was your plan for the ironworks and the way you showed it off that convinced him to make his recommendation. If you hadn't impressed him, he never would have proposed canceling that big payment, no matter what Fred thought of you."

Those expressive blue eyes met hers, and for the first time she could recall, they were dark with uncertainty. "You really believe that?"

"Without question." Nodding to emphasize her point, she searched for a way to convince him. "Remember, I've worked with lots of lawyers and banking types. They make their decisions based on logic, not sentiment. Rick considers the forge a good risk, and that's why he's going to bat for you. Period, end of story."

Apparently satisfied, Brian rubbed the shoulder that had just gotten such a workout, closing his eyes as he sighed at the ceiling. She recognized the gesture as a silent prayer, and she waited for him to look at her again.

"You realize what it means if I get until the end of the summer to pay off this loan?" he asked.

She knew where he was headed, and she fielded the question with a smile. "Your monthly payment will go down."

"Yeah. What're we gonna do with all that money?"

"Tuck it away for a rainy day," she replied without thinking. It was crazy, since not long ago, her first thought would have been using the windfall to increase her paltry salary. In that moment, she realized that sometime in the past couple of weeks, she'd decided that she wanted to be part of Liberty Creek Forge beyond the next few months.

Smart or foolish, she was in this for the long haul. And it felt wonderful.

It had been a long time since Brian had bothered to do anything on Valentine's Day.

Sure, he scoffed at the holiday invented by florists, jewelers and candy companies in a thinly veiled attempt to separate men from a chunk of their hard-earned money. But this one was different, and while he finished getting dressed, an odd thought entered his mind.

How did you go about taking a friend to a dance?

Brian had never even considered doing such a thing, so he wasn't sure of the etiquette. But his male common sense told him that, friend or not, Lindsay was a woman and probably wouldn't object to a little pampering. After all she'd been through, he firmly believed she deserved it.

So on his way to pick her up, he stopped in at the little boutique that sold flowers along with books, newspapers and an array of quirky New England souvenirs. Strolling past the knickknacks that were meant to appeal to tourists, he found the owner at the back counter, finishing up a phone call.

"I'm sorry, sir, but I'm all out of red roses." There was a pause, and Christy gave Brian an apologetic smile while she listened. He couldn't hear anything the caller was saying, but by the tone that filtered out to him from the receiver, the poor guy was desperate. "You could try the shop in Waterford, but at this late hour on Valentine's Day, they may give you the same answer. I hope things work out for you. Goodbye."

"Desperate?" Brian asked.

"And how." Leaning on the counter, she laughed. "Can you believe he forgot it was Valentine's Day?"

"Does he live in a cave?"

"I know—right? Anyway, what can I do for you?"

Brian figured that by now, the local gossips had paired him off with his new office manager, so he didn't bother shuffling around the issue. "Lindsay and I are going to the Sweetheart Dance tonight. I need something she'll like. Any ideas?"

The florist pursed her lips in obvious disapproval, and he cocked his head at her. "Come on, Christy. Not you, too. High school was a long time ago."

"That may be, but judging by her current state, she hasn't changed a bit. You can do so much better than her."

A wave of bitterness threatened to break free, and

Brian managed to contain it, but it was a near thing. Turning on his heel, he stalked back the way he'd come.

"Don't you want some flowers?"

"Not from you," he snarled without turning around.

When he got to the door, he just about ripped it off his hinges on his way out. The sound of jangling bells slamming against the glass was satisfying but not nearly enough to cool him off.

He had a little extra time now, and he used it to walk off some of the temper that had spiked so unexpectedly. He'd spent a lot of time in high school defending the pretty outsider from anyone who dared to run her down. It wasn't her fault that she was the daughter of the town flirt, and he'd never been able to understand why so many of their classmates assumed that Lindsay would follow in her mom's questionable footsteps.

Brian was pretty even-keeled by nature, but for some reason, whenever someone went after Lindsay, he just about lost his mind. For all the maturing he'd done, it seemed that the instinct to protect her ran so deep inside him, he hadn't outgrown it yet. He had the feeling that meant something—something important—but he was too agitated to work it through at the moment. Right now, he needed to focus on regaining his usual cool so his very perceptive office manager wouldn't suspect that something was wrong.

After a few minutes, he felt like he had ahold of his temper again, and he circled back to his truck to drive the short distance to Gran's house. Taking a deep breath, he rang the bell and stepped back, hands folded in front of him in a casual pose he hoped was convincing.

The second that Lindsay saw him, he knew he hadn't walked for long enough.

"What's wrong?" she demanded, brow furrowing in concern.

"Nothing. Why?"

Reaching out, she rested one of her slender hands on his, which had curled into fists without him noticing. When those incredible eyes met his, the worry in them made him want to take her in his arms the way he had the night of the dance committee meeting, when she'd turned to him for comfort. In that moment, lit by the antique coach lights on his grandmother's front porch, she looked more beautiful than ever, and he finally understood what had been going on with him.

Despite his best efforts to keep her at a distance, he'd gone and fallen in love with Lindsay Holland all over again.

It was the worst possible thing that could've happened, and somehow, he had to get through this evening without letting her see it. Swallowing a groan of frustration, he plastered a careless grin on his face. "No biggie. It's kinda cold and my snowmobiling gloves don't exactly go with this coat."

"Which looks very nice on you, by the way," she complimented him as she opened the inner door for him.

In the foyer, she gave him a long, assessing look and opened her mouth to say something before quickly closing it. Turning away, she took her coat from the rack and got into one sleeve fairly easily. She groped for the other one, and it occurred to him that she honestly couldn't stretch around far enough to reach it.

"Here, let me," he said, holding it where she could maneuver into it.

"Thank you. It seems like I get less flexible every day."

"No problem."

Putting her hands around her hair, she let it cascade over her shoulders in a waterfall of dark curls that snared his attention as if he'd never seen anything like that before. At work, she wore her hair pulled back out of the way, and he'd gotten accustomed to seeing her that way. With it framing her face, she had a softer, more delicate appearance that was doing funky things to his suddenly active heart.

It was the holiday, he reasoned as he escorted her out to his truck. It was tough to stay neutral when you'd been bombarded with romantic messages for the past month. Fortunately for him, this wasn't a date, and he didn't have to worry about impressing Lindsay. Because quite honestly, he was so out of sorts, he didn't trust himself to handle much more than small talk.

When they pulled in at the school, the place was lit up like a resort, and the front parking lot was already filled to near bursting.

"This is awesome," she approved, eyes sparkling in delight. "The early ticket sales were encouraging, but Holly warned me that some folks might donate and not actually attend the event. It's great to see so many people here."

"Adding the kids' party was a stroke of genius," he told her as he pulled into the nearest spot he could find. "That made it easy for parents to get some grown-up time together without having to hire a babysitter."

"I'm just glad it worked out. I really wanted to do something to help raise the money we need." She angled a shy look at him. "You probably think it's silly, but I love that bridge."

In a heartbeat, Brian was back in high school, one

arm around Lindsay and the other dangling over the railing while they stood on the walkway and tossed pebbles into the rushing creek below. Smiling at the memory, he shook his head. "I don't think it's silly at all. We had some nice times there, didn't we?"

"Some of my best ever." After a few moments, she gave him the kind of sad smile that he'd seen on her face too many times. "Actually, the best. You always made me feel like I was the only girl in the world. I just wish I'd appreciated you more when I had you."

You still have me, he nearly blurted before he caught himself. Muting his response into something less desperate-sounding, he said, "What do you say we go have some punch and see if we remember those waltzing lessons they tormented us with in gym class?"

That got him the laugh he'd been after, and she took his arm as they went up the wide sidewalk to the front door. Emma's art students had outdone themselves, and their handiwork met the guests who were strolling through the archway adorned with ropes of green twine strung through crepe paper flowers of every shade of pink and red he'd ever seen. Music played over the loudspeakers, and he recognized a fairly recent ballad that had people humming along while they strolled toward the gym.

He and Lindsay stopped to check on things in the cafeteria, where tables were set up for snacks and kid-friendly prizes that had been donated by local shops. Brian noticed everything from music gift cards, DVDs and the old classic: baskets full of candy.

"This is awesome," he commented with a chuckle. "When we do this kinda thing at church, folks usually donate books and board games."

"I put Holly and a couple of moms in charge of collecting everything," Lindsay explained. "I figured they know what their kids like, so they'd know what would appeal to the different age groups."

"Smart."

"Thank you." Looking around, she smiled. "Everyone looks like they're having a good time."

"What's not to like? There's a big popcorn cart in the cafeteria."

"That was Hal Rogers's idea. It's his machine, too. He said his grandchildren love movie theater popcorn, so he invested in a commercial cart last year. He brings it to all their family events, and he's very popular."

"I don't doubt it."

Out in the hallway, several people greeted him, and Brian felt Lindsay stiffen reflexively beside him. Not everyone was thrilled to have her back in Liberty Creek, and after Christy had insulted her outright, he could only imagine what she'd been hearing around town.

"Lindsay, what a pretty dress," Sharon Rogers complimented her, adding a quick hug. "That shade of blue is perfect for you."

"Thank you," she replied, clearly pleased by the warm reception. "I have to hand it to you and the decorating committee. You did a fabulous job in the kids' area."

Sharon winked. "Wait till you see the gym. I don't mind saying we knocked it out of the park in there." Someone was waving to her, and she returned the gesture. "That's my cousin, and she doesn't know anyone here. I'll catch up with you later."

Music and laughter filtered out into the main hallway, and as Brian escorted Lindsay into the gym, he stopped dead in his tracks. The only word he could think of was *wow*.

If it weren't for the basketball nets that had been levered back against the ceiling, he never would've known he was standing in a high school gymnasium. White lattice stood against the walls, and in each section there were places for people to write notes or pin up the photos a photographer was taking and printing out for couples on his printer.

Long tables full of refreshments lined one wall, holding a range of finger foods, drinks and desserts. He recognized several of Gran's specialties, and made a beeline for one of the platters that was already half empty.

"What are you doing?" Lindsay demanded, a little breathless from rushing after him.

In answer, he plucked two of the heart-shaped red velvet cupcakes from their stand and held one out for her. After her first bite, she hummed in appreciation. "Okay, now I get it. These are amazing."

"And really popular at the bakery. Trust me—if you come back in a few minutes, there will be nothing but crumbs on that plate."

"That wouldn't surprise me in the least." Eyes sparkling with humor, she said, "Speaking of plates, though, we should probably go back to the head of the line and get some."

Chuckling at the gentle scolding, he motioned for her to go in front of him. "Yeah, I guess. Lost my head there for a second."

"Totally understandable."

Once they had their snacks, they found a set of chairs at a table and sat down to take in the event at a more leisurely pace.

"So," Lindsay began, "who did you leave your side-kick with tonight?"

"He's over at Sam and Holly's. I don't think big brother's too happy, though. Chase has been begging them for a puppy since Christmas, and hanging out with such a fun dog isn't gonna make it any easier for them to keep telling him no."

"Have you gotten any calls about your lost-dog fly-ers?"

Brian frowned. "Not a single one. I even put an ad in the newspaper, but I haven't heard anything. Either Riley's former owner moved away, or they don't miss him enough to go out looking for him. Whichever it is, I feel bad for the little guy."

Lindsay gave him a long, suspicious look. "You're thinking about keeping him, aren't you?"

"Folks wants puppies, not full-grown dogs. There's a humane shelter near here, and I know they'd take good care of him, but it's not the same as belonging to a fam-ily." He blew out a breath. "As great as he is, I hate the thought of him being stuck there for months, getting excited when people come through, and then not being adopted. At least if he stays with me, I can bring him to work so he's not alone all day. As long as you don't mind him hanging out in the office with you."

"He's very well behaved, and I like having him around, so it's not a problem for me." She rewarded him with an approving smile. "You look all rugged and tough, but underneath all that swagger, you're just a big ol' softy."

"Yeah, well, don't spread that around. I've got a rep-utation to protect."

"No problem. Even if I knew anyone I'd want to tell, they probably wouldn't believe me." Leaning back in her chair, Lindsay's eyes roamed around the decorated walls with obvious approval. "Sharon was right about what a fabulous job they did in here. Between the streamers, the lights and that huge mirrored ball spinning around, it reminds me of when we went to the prom in high school."

"I was just thinking the same thing," Brian confessed with a grin. Standing in front of her, he grinned and held out his hand. "So, Holland—you wanna dance?"

From the exuberant laugh she let out, he knew that she recognized the line from the night she'd been reminiscing about. Resting her hands on her rounded stomach, she cautioned, "I'm afraid you won't be able to get as close to me as you did back then."

Quite honestly, Brian thought that was probably for the best. His feelings for Lindsay had always been complicated, and now they seemed to be more tangled up than ever. One minute, he had no trouble viewing her as strictly his business partner, and the next he caught himself wondering if there might be a chance for something more between them.

One thing was still the same, though. Lindsay Holland came loaded down with a lot of baggage, and with everything he had going on these days, he wasn't sure that he was in a position to drop everything he'd been juggling and shoulder her burdens along with his own.

So that left him going one step forward, one step back. Drawn to her in a way he still didn't comprehend, leery of making a commitment to her and her baby that he might not be able to keep. Basically, he kept ending up at the same place he'd been in when he started. It was frustrating, to say the least.

But for now, he shoved all that uncertainty aside and

focused on giving the mom-to-be some much-needed fun. "That's okay. We'll figure it out."

For some reason, she tilted her head in the pose that always made him suspect that she saw more of him than the average person did. Intelligence sparked in those incredible blue eyes, and she slowly rose to join him in a corner of the polished floor. He held her loosely in his arms, keeping her at a nice, respectable distance.

It was still close enough for him to catch the scent of her perfume, and he let out a mental groan. A light spray of something floral, it made him think of picnics on summer days, in spite of the fact that it was about ten degrees and there was four feet of snow piled up outside.

"Brian?"

Yanking his attention back to the gorgeous woman in front of him, he forced a casual expression. "Yeah?"

"Were you referring to something besides dancing earlier?"

Busted. He should have known better than to suggest something that would put them in such close contact with each other. She read him too well for him to successfully evade her for long. "When?"

"When you mentioned us figuring out how to dance. You had a strange look on your face, and I was wondering if you meant it another way."

His mind raced for a plausible way to explain the reaction even he didn't understand. When it came up empty, he punted. "What other way is there?"

"I don't know," she shot back, temper glittering in her eyes. "That's why I asked. Forget I said anything."

She didn't storm off, but he could feel her pulling away from him, as if she was getting ready to bolt as soon as the song ended. Brian felt terrible for spoiling her one evening out in months, and he tucked his pride away to apologize.

"Lindsay, I'm sorry. I didn't mean to make you mad, but I don't know how to answer your question."

"It was simple enough," she pointed out curtly. "Yes or no would've done it."

The DJ started another song, and she was still glaring up at him instead of storming off the way he'd expected. He took that as a good sign. Some of the tension he'd felt in her had eased, and he drew her as close as he dared. A variety of explanations tumbled through his mind, but in the end he wisely chose the one that he felt would cause them both the least amount of trouble.

"Mostly, I was thinking about how we've learned to do things together since you started working at the forge. We even figured out how to pull together this thing," he added, motioning at the couples around them. "We make a pretty good team."

She studied him with the skeptical look he'd come to expect whenever he caught this very guarded woman by surprise. "You sound like you weren't expecting that."

"I wasn't," he admitted, happily veering away from what could have been a prickly—and far too personal— conversation. "We're both so stubborn, I wasn't sure how it'd go when we disagreed."

"Which is most of the time," she pointed out with a smirk. "If you'd just do what I tell you to, there'd be a lot less arguing."

"Aw, what fun would that be?"

She laughed, but the next moment, she grew pensive. "How is it that no matter what's going on in my messed-up life, you can always make me laugh?"

"It's a gift," he replied smoothly, hoping to coax a

smile from her. When she looked down in an obvious attempt to avoid him, he ducked his head for a closer look. The tears shimmering on her cheeks washed away his amusement, and he felt his grip on her tighten all on its own. "What's wrong?"

"Nothing," she answered in a watery voice, wiping away the tears. Taking a long breath, she straightened to meet his gaze in the direct way he'd always admired. "Really, nothing. Last night, I cried at a puppy food commercial. Stupid, right?"

"Isn't being extra emotional part of the mom-to-be package?"

"I guess."

"Then it's not stupid. I'm just glad there's nothing seriously wrong. The women's clinic is really nice, but I'm not keen on going back there anytime soon."

His comment earned him another head tilt, and he braced himself for more surprises. This woman had a knack for doing that to him, and he'd learned to expect the unexpected from her.

"Brian, I know it's asking a lot," she began in a hesitant tone that nearly broke his heart. Lindsay had become so accustomed to not relying on anyone, he could only imagine how terrifying it was to face the birth of her child on her own.

"You can ask me anything, Lindsay. If I can do it, I will."

This time, it was gratitude that flooded those amazing blue eyes. "You're so wonderful to me. I don't know what I did to deserve someone like you."

"You don't have to do anything," he assured her gently, brushing a stray lock of curls back over her shoulder. "You never did."

He hadn't meant to say those last few words out loud, and he cringed inwardly, waiting to see how she'd react. Neither of them had expressed the least interest in revisiting the relationship they once had, and he wasn't about to suggest it now. The future was already far too unsettled.

"You're the sweetest, most generous guy I've ever met," she said, beaming up at him like he was Superman. "I was hoping that when it comes time to drive to the hospital, you'd be the one to take me. I know they'll send an ambulance, but I'm probably going to be terrified, and it would be so nice to have you there."

"Of course I will."

"You don't have to be in the delivery room or anything," she clarified hastily. "You don't even have to wait around if you don't want to. This isn't your baby, so I'll understand if you'd rather not be involved that way."

Brian understood just how difficult it was for her to ask anyone for help. He also knew that she fully expected to be disappointed by—well, everyone. Pulling a serious face, he asked, "So you want me to drop you at the front desk like a hamper full of laundry and then drive home?"

"I—" Her astonished look quickly morphed into laughter, which had been his intent. "When you say it like that, it sounds pretty ridiculous."

"Good, 'cause it is. If you don't want me in the delivery room, that's fine. But I'll be waiting around, so if you change your mind, just send them out for me. I'll be there."

"Even if it takes all night?"

"Even if." Gently grasping her shoulders, he made sure he had her full attention. "You're not alone in this,

Lindsay. My family and I will all be here to support you. Both of you."

Her chin began trembling, and she took a moment to compose herself before gazing up at him with grateful eyes. "Thank you."

"Anytime."

"I'm going to hold you to that," she retorted, making it sound an awful lot like a threat.

"Yeah," he teased, giving her a quick hug. "I figured you would."

Chapter Nine

It had been quite the week.

Lindsay snuggled down in the soft bed early Sunday morning, cozy and warm under the quilt that Great-grandma Calhoun had made ages ago. Outside the windows she could see that last night's blizzard had finally moved on, and the sky was a clear, sunny blue. The frost on the panes told her it was still pretty cold out there, though, and she considered following her usual sleep-in approach to Sundays.

She was in the final month of her pregnancy, and from her expectant mother book she knew that her daughter was growing at a crazy rate. Putting on weight, getting ready to come out and greet the world.

For the millionth time, she acknowledged that she had very limited exposure to children in general. Sam and Holly's son, Chase, was a great kid, and she enjoyed spending time with him, but she had no idea what it took to raise a child. Philosophically, she was prepared to do whatever was necessary to give her own little one a good life, but in truth she had no clue what that meant.

A tendril of doubt slithered around her like an invisible python, making it hard for her to breathe. *Panic attack*, she told herself sternly, raising herself to a partial sitting position to take deep breaths and calm her racing heart.

Breathe in, breathe out, she silently coached herself, relieved when the wave of terror receded enough for her to relax a bit. The commotion had apparently woken the baby, who gave her a hearty kick that knocked the air out of her lungs. No matter what position she tried, the squirming continued, so she finally threw off the covers and stood up. Massaging her stomach to calm her fractious passenger, she decided a little motherly reassurance was in order.

"I know it's tough, being all cramped in there. We're just going to have to make the best of it." The sound of her voice seemed to be helping, so she kept going. "It's not much longer now, and you'll finally be here. I can't wait to hold you, see how big and strong you've gotten. Those sonogram pictures are nice, but it's not the same as seeing you for myself."

There was a soft knock on the door, and she opened it to find Ellie in the hallway. "Is everything all right, dear?"

"Oh, fine. Just chatting with the baby, the way they recommend in my book," she explained, hoping she didn't sound like a complete loon.

"I've heard that, too. Just so you know, they like the sound of their mother's voice, no matter how old they get."

"That's good to know."

Smiling, Ellie patted her arm in a reassuring gesture. "I've no doubt you'll do just fine, once you get the hang of mothering."

"I hope so."

"The family's coming over for lunch after church. You're welcome to join us if you feel up to it."

"I knew I smelled something amazing coming from the kitchen," Lindsay commented with a smile. "I'd love to see everyone."

"Wonderful! I'll be driving over to the chapel in a little while. Can I get you anything before I leave?"

"No, but thank you." An idea popped into her head, and it felt so right, she decided to go with it. "Could I go to church with you?"

Ellie beamed as if she'd suggested they take a whirlwind trip to Paris. "Of course, you can. I'd love to have the company."

"Company?" Lindsay repeated, laughing. "You make it sound like you'd be sitting in the pew all by yourself if I wasn't with you. Your whole family will be there."

"Yes, but not you." Grasping her arms, Ellie pulled her into a warm hug, then held her out for another approving smile. "I hope you don't mind me saying this, but I've been praying that you'd decide to come with me one of these Sundays. I'm thrilled that it's today."

The feelings that seemed to be bubbling way too close to the surface lately threatened to swamp her in an embarrassing rush of tears. Doing that to Brian at the dance had been bad enough. She didn't want to put his lovely grandmother through it, too. Swallowing hard, she steadied her voice before speaking. "Ellie, you've been so incredible through all this. Giving me a place to stay, making such great meals, praying for me. How can I ever thank you?"

"By having a beautiful, healthy child, and raising her to be the kind of person this world needs more of. And being happy yourself," she added with a sage look that was comforting and cautioning all at once. "Trust me, if you have those, you'll have a good life."

Because it was Ellie, Lindsay accepted the advice without reservation. "I'll try."

"Good for you. Now, I'll go whip us up some breakfast while you get ready."

After another quick hug, she left Lindsay in the upstairs hallway. While she showered and picked out one of the nicer dresses that Holly had loaned her, it struck her that since coming back to Liberty Creek, she'd been shown more affection than she'd gotten in months. She rarely thought of Jeff anymore, and now it made sense why.

He hadn't loved her. He'd wanted her with him, and he'd always relished showing her off to his friends. But now she understood that wasn't love. It was possession. Immature and boastful, Jeff had shown her a great time for a while, but in the long run, he'd proven that he couldn't be trusted when things got tough.

Not like Brian, she thought with a smile in the mirror. Time and again, he'd come to her rescue, in big ways and little ones. Always there, standing behind her in case she needed him. The forge was his business, but he allowed her to run the office and website her own way, trusting her to do what was best for his company. On a personal note, his gallant offer to hold her hand throughout her upcoming labor still amazed her, because she couldn't imagine any other guy she'd known doing the same.

Somehow, he'd found a way to forgive her for the awful way she'd treated him in the past and become her friend. No matter what happened to her in the future, she'd never forget what he did to help her when she was at her most vulnerable.

Following a light breakfast, she and Ellie drove through a smattering of flurries to church. Lindsay hadn't been there since the town meeting about the bridge, and while that visit had turned out well enough, for some reason she felt nervous now. Then she saw Brian's four-by-four parked in the lot, and her anxiety eased a bit. If anyone looked askance at a single pregnant woman showing up for worship, she was confident that the no-nonsense owner of Liberty Creek Forge would set them straight.

The Calhoun crew was sitting together in a pew near the center of the chapel, chatting with people around them while they waited for the service to start. Brian glanced toward the doorway, and his face broke into a broad grin when he saw her. He stood as she and Ellie approached, and Lindsay couldn't help smiling back as he and Sam moved into the aisle to let them in.

"Such a gentleman," she teased him, taking her seat next to Holly.

"Showing off for you," his sister-in-law murmured, glancing over to where he and Sam were talking in construction terms. Something about sistering beams and building pony walls, which Lindsay didn't begin to understand.

"I can't imagine why," she confided, although she had to admit the idea appealed to her more than it should have.

"Don't get me wrong—Brian's a terrific guy," Holly clarified in a hushed tone. "But once he came back from Portsmouth, he didn't seem interested in anything other than getting the ironworks up and running again. Until you got here."

She added a knowing look, and Lindsay couldn't keep back a laugh. "I think I follow you, but you've got it wrong. Brian's been a good friend and a great boss, but that's it. We have way too much history to be anything more."

"You sound unhappy about that."

Truthfully, Lindsay wasn't sure how she felt about it. While she understood the reasons for them to remain at a distance from each other, there was a tiny part of her that wished it could be different. Shrugging, she said, "It is what it is. You know?"

"Yes, I do. So, how are you and your little one doing these days?"

"Fine."

Holly gave her a long look, and Lindsay relented with a sigh. "One minute, I'm fine, the next I'm blubbering like a baby. Does that ever go away?"

"The first time you hold her, you'll feel incredible," the experienced mom replied with a fond smile at Chase. "That's when you know for sure that all the trouble was worth it."

Lindsay still had no idea how she'd cope with raising a child all by herself, but given the bond she already felt with her daughter, it wasn't hard to envision loving her at first sight. That kind of responsibility wasn't going to be easy to carry, though, and she leaned closer to make certain that no one could hear her. "Holly, can I ask you something really personal?"

"About being a mom, you mean?" At Lindsay's nod, she smiled. "Go ahead."

"Ellie told me you were a widow and you raised Chase mostly by yourself. How on earth did you manage?"

"Three things. Patience, determination and a whole lot of faith. Beyond that, I had good friends around me, and a family that supported me when things got tough. And then, when we came here, we met Sam. He filled in all the things we'd been missing."

She smiled over at her husband, and even though he was midsentence, he paused long enough to grin back before continuing his discussion with Brian.

"It can't be easy to find a guy who's willing to be a father to another man's child."

"I wouldn't know, because I never actually tried. Sam was a blessing I didn't ask for, and that made him all the more special."

Lindsay had run out of questions, but Holly's comment about blessings got her thinking. Was it possible for her—the illegitimate child of a shameless flirt—to be blessed that way? Because of her own difficult upbringing, she believed that children weren't to blame for their parents' missteps, and she hoped other people would be open-minded enough to give her daughter a chance despite her questionable start.

Lindsay acknowledged that some people in the conservative little town were chilly toward her, and she'd done her best to shrug off their disapproval of her. But the Calhouns, along with many others, seemed to be unconcerned with her shady background. They'd given her an opportunity to prove herself, and she'd done her best to show that she deserved their trust.

Was it possible that God could overlook her flaws, too?

"By the way," Holly continued, "if you decide you'd

like a coach in the delivery room with you, just call me. I'll meet you at the hospital, no matter what time it is."

Lindsay's jaw fell open in shock. "Seriously?"

"Very seriously. Brian's sweet, and I know he'd do whatever he could, but it's not the same as having someone there with you who's been through it before. It's up to you, but I'd be happy to help out if you want me there."

"Thank you," Lindsay replied, still unable to believe what she'd heard. "I've seen videos about what's coming, so I just might take you up on that."

The sound of the organist warming up broke into their conversation, and people who'd been milling around quickly found their seats. Brian slid in beside her, giving her a quick smile. "Morning, gorgeous."

It was a common greeting he'd used for her in high school, and she laughed quietly. "That's one I haven't heard in a while. You're in a good mood."

"That's 'cause Sam's gonna help me knock out those building repairs this week. Now that we're actually in business, I figure we oughta do some general maintenance and put a big window in the office so you don't feel like you're working in a shoe box."

"That sounds good, but you don't have to do all that for me. I'm fine in there."

"Anyway," he continued as if she hadn't said anything, "we'll be making a real mess, so you should plan on working from Gran's until we're finished."

She picked up the hymnal and turned to the first song listed on the board up front. "I should be able to get most things done from there. I certainly won't miss fighting with that old space heater to get it running. It's not as reliable as it could be."

"Man, are you picky."

She made a face at him, and he laughed as he stood to join in the singing. When she tried to do the same, she discovered that she couldn't quite manage it in the confined space. Without a word, he reached down and helped her to her feet. Feeling her face heat with embarrassment, she murmured her thanks.

"Anytime." He punctuated his reply with one of his charmingly crooked grins, which she couldn't help returning.

Simple and reassuring, his response chased her discomfort away, and it occurred to her that this wasn't the first time. As if that wasn't enough, she knew that he honestly meant it, because that was the sort of man Brian Calhoun was.

A wave of emotion washed over her, and she struggled to keep her composure so no one would notice her over-the-top reaction to his chivalrous gesture. Brian's strength was tempered by a kind, caring nature and a heart that was probably too big for his own good. Not long ago, when she'd run out of options, returning here had seemed like choosing to take a dead-end road that led back to the sad past she'd once been so eager to leave behind. But now, she couldn't imagine going anywhere else.

After a lifetime of searching, on the other side of an old-fashioned covered bridge, she'd finally found the place where she truly belonged. What an amazing turn of events this was.

When Brian's arm settled around her shoulders, she realized she'd unconsciously leaned against him. He gave a little squeeze, and when she looked up, he mouthed, "Okay?"

In that moment, she felt confident that things were going to work out for her. Smiling up at him, she nodded, and he rewarded her with a proud look before letting his hand fall back to his side.

And, for the first time in her life, Lindsay closed her eyes to pray.

Thank You, God, for bringing me home.

A sensation of warmth enveloped her, and the only explanation she could come up with was that He was reaching down to her from heaven, welcoming her into His house. The gratitude she felt was almost overwhelming, but in a good way. All these years, the thing she'd been missing was right in front of her. All she had to do was accept what He was offering her. For someone who'd always scraped and fought for what she got, it was a heady concept.

While she was mulling that over, she realized that Pastor Welch had begun speaking. No one around her seemed to have noticed her lack of attention to the sermon, and she put her epiphany aside to focus on the preacher. Most of what he was saying didn't make much sense to her, but one section in particular resonated with her immediately.

"When we go astray," he told them in a voice that clearly said he'd done it himself, "we have two choices—keep going down that wrong path, or change course and head back in the right direction. Sometimes that means we have to retrace steps that are painful for us, endure memories that we'd rather not go through again. But if we have the courage to do that, we may find what we're looking for on a path that we once thought was a dead end."

He'd so perfectly nailed what Lindsay had just been

thinking, it was all she could do to keep her jaw from dropping open in shock. Stealing glances at others in the congregation, she noticed some of them nodding, as if they also saw themselves in his simple, homespun advice. Several smiles clued her in that their own back-tracking had worked out well for them, giving her even more hope that her unfamiliar bout of positivity wasn't merely wishful thinking.

Finding that truth here, in this simple New Hampshire chapel, struck her as the perfect way to start a new future for her and the little girl she was bringing into the world.

"And now," the pastor announced proudly, "as secretary of the town council, I've been given the fun job of letting you all know the results of our recent fund-raising efforts. Thanks to Lindsay Holland, her devoted committee and all those who attended, the Sweetheart Dance was a rousing success. Every dollar earned will go toward the remaining repairs, and if the weather cooperates, our lovely new bridge will be ready for traffic—and tourists—at the beginning of April."

The entire group applauded and cheered, turning in their seats to congratulate each other on a job well-done. Lindsay accepted her share of the praise, which made her eventful morning all the more meaningful to her. Having suffered through years of sidelong looks and thinly veiled insults as a teenager, it was wonderful to feel accepted and valued for what she'd done to help the town.

When the service was over, some people filed toward the door, while others hung back to discuss their plans for the day.

"We'll see you all over at Ellie's," Brian's mother,

Melinda, reminded them before dashing after their hostess, who was already long gone.

The rest of the family mingled with their neighbors, laughing and catching up on the latest news from the forge. Local residents showed a great deal of interest in Brian's new venture, and he went out of his way to include her in those conversations.

That feeling of belonging here remained strong, and Lindsay's mood brightened as she made her way out with Brian behind her. Ellie often had the family over for lunch after church, and Lindsay had always joined them. But today, she felt more like she deserved her spot at the family gathering than she had before.

"That's a pretty big smile," Brian commented as he walked her to his truck.

"It's a pretty nice day," she replied, taking in a deep breath of fresh, chilly air. "It sounds crazy, but on a morning like this, I feel like anything could happen."

"Good things, I hope."

"Only good things," she assured him as he opened the passenger door and helped her up into the cab. Once he settled in beside her, she turned to him and asked, "What do you think of 'Taylor'?"

Typical Brian, he didn't blank out on her and ask who Taylor was. Instead, he cocked his head and grinned. "Taylor Holland. Sounds like a little girl who's gonna make the world a better place just by being in it."

"Not 'Tay,' though," Lindsay clarified. "I always hated being called 'Lin.'"

"Yeah, I remember," he commented, chuckling as he started the engine.

"You never did that, though. It was one of the things I liked best about you back then."

"What about now?"

There were so many qualities she admired, but one stuck out above the others, and she smiled. "That you care about me, and a little girl you've never even met."

"I always cared, Lindsay," he informed her as he pulled into Ellie's driveway. Parking the truck, he swiveled to face her with an intense look unlike any she'd ever gotten from him. "I never stopped."

"Really?"

"I used to wonder where you were," he confided with a sigh, glancing out the grimy windshield before meeting her eyes again. "If you were safe, and happy. If you ever thought about me."

Fondness sparkled in those deep blue eyes, taking her back to the days when he'd been her hero, defending her from anyone who dared to treat her with anything less than the respect he believed she deserved. And that was when she knew.

She loved Brian Calhoun, she realized now. In all honesty, she always had, and she wasn't entirely certain that she'd ever stopped.

"That was outta line," he said tersely. "I apologize."

He didn't offer anything more as he helped her down and got her safely to Ellie's front door. Lindsay had no clue what to say, so she kept quiet, hoping the awkward moment would pass and they could enjoy a pleasant lunch with his family.

When they paused in the foyer, her eyes were drawn to the living room, which was decked out in pink balloons and streamers, with a pile of gifts wrapped in every shade of pink she'd ever seen.

"What's this?" she asked him.

"Looks like a party to me," he replied, any trace of their earlier exchange gone.

Ellie appeared in the kitchen doorway wearing an apron proclaiming her the Best Grandma Ever, and Lindsay asked, "For me?"

"And the little one who's on her way," the sweet lady said with a smile. "You'll be needing some things for her, and we thought it would be nice to make a celebration of it."

"Oh, Ellie," Lindsay gasped, embracing her tightly before pulling away. "Thank you so much. You have no idea how much this means to me."

Between this and Holly volunteering to coach her in the delivery room, Lindsay thought she just might burst from sheer happiness. She couldn't recall ever feeling that way, and the strength of those emotions threatened to swamp her self-control for the umpteenth time this week.

"Puppies?" Brian murmured into her ear.

Swallowing hard, she nodded. "And kittens and baby otters. All this affection is a lot for me to process, I guess."

"Are you planning to stick around here for a while?"

The question dovetailed so perfectly with the realization she'd come to during the service, she couldn't help smiling. "Yes."

"Then you'd better get used to it. My family likes you, and this is how it's gonna be."

Added to the revelation he'd made earlier, the matter-of-fact declaration sent a warm current through her from head to toe. She wasn't well-acquainted with the kind of unconditional love that the Calhouns had showered on her, so it might take her a while to get comfortable with it.

Discovering that she still had such strong feelings for Brian had been unsettling, because she'd thought she'd left all that behind her years ago. She didn't know how things might work out between them this time, but she'd always be grateful to him for giving her another chance.

Working from home was fabulous.

Especially when you were in your last month of pregnancy and getting around got a little tougher every day. Lindsay had set herself up in the living room, cozied up next to the fire, alternating data entry with responding to orders as they came in. Her goal was to respond to customers within five minutes so they'd know there was a real live person on the other end instead of some robot in a warehouse.

In a rare meeting of the minds, she and Brian had agreed that the specialized nature of Liberty Creek Forge's products demanded kid-glove treatment of people who contacted them. Because of that, she was determined to make every one of them feel as special as humanly possible. Her cell phone was the contact number on the website, and when it rang, she answered in her usual professional greeting.

"Good morning, this is Liberty Creek Forge. My name is Lindsay. How may I help you?"

"I'm on your website right now and I'm curious about the size options on that beautiful wine rack," a woman's voice explained. "Could you make something other than the two listed on the page?"

"Absolutely. Would you like it bigger or smaller?"

"Bigger. We run a small vineyard in Vermont, and I'd like to use some of them in our tasting room."

She read off the dimensions, and Lindsay gave the answer Brian had always insisted she use. "Our master forger can make anything you need. How many would you like?"

"Ten."

Lindsay nearly swallowed her tongue. This was the biggest order they'd gotten to date, and she waited a beat to make sure her voice wouldn't come out in an excited squeak. "Did you have a specific delivery date in mind?"

"As soon as possible." The woman laughed. "I guess you hear that a lot, but in this case it's for real. We've got a spring event scheduled for mid-April, and I'd love to have them installed and filled in time for that."

Lindsay didn't hesitate to make the commitment, since she was confident Brian would work night and day to have the shipment ready in time. She arranged for a down payment of half the fee, then completed the order and emailed the details to their first big customer.

And then she called Brian. She relayed the stellar news, and he blew out a long breath. "Okay, I can do that."

"Good, because that's what I told her."

He didn't scold her for not checking with him first, just laughed. "Why am I not surprised?"

"You want the forge to succeed, right?"

"More than anything."

"You'll make that happen by being light on your feet," she informed him. "Large companies can't adjust their production runs for specialty items like this. You can, and that gives you an advantage over them.

Once people see for themselves how great your products are, they'll tell their friends, and then you'll have even more business."

"Are you angling for a raise?"

"No, but I'm hoping that someday when the books aren't always in the red, you might decide I've earned one."

"You already have," he told her in a sincere tone. "I just wish I was able to give it to you."

She hadn't meant to make him feel guilty, and she hunted for a way to let him off the hook without making things worse. "When you can afford to fix the furnace in your own house, we'll talk about increasing my salary."

"Deal. Since we're on the phone, is there anything else we need to go over?"

She'd just started walking him through the items on her list when the front doorbell rang. She groaned at the unappealing thought of leaving her comfy seat on the couch. "Who could that be? Everyone in town knows Ellie's at the bakery this time of day."

"Ignore it. They'll go away."

She kept quiet, hoping he was right. Instead, the visitor rang again, pressing the button in a quick succession that made it clear they weren't giving up anytime soon. "I'd better go answer it."

"Go ahead. I'm not going anywhere, so just call me back when you're done."

Grumbling to no one in particular, Lindsay switched off her phone and set it on the side table. With a significant effort, she levered herself up to go into the foyer. Peering through the sidelight, she couldn't believe her eyes. Blinking, she looked again just to be sure she'd seen right.

Sliding the dead bolt, she opened the outer door half-way, ready to slam it shut if the mood struck her. "Jeff, what are you doing here?"

"I'm so glad I found you," he replied, neatly sidestepping her question. "The clerk at the post office said you were staying here. I was visiting some of our old friends in Cleveland, and I came as soon as I heard about the baby. How are you doing?"

"Fine. Thanks for stopping by."

She started to shut the door, but he stopped it with his hand. "I have to talk to you, but it's freezing out here. Can I come in?"

"No."

The classically handsome face that masked such a devious mind twisted in an expression that looked a lot like remorse. "I deserve that, and I don't blame you."

"How nice."

"This might change your mind about me, though." He reached a leather-gloved hand into the pocket of his designer dress coat and pulled out an envelope. When she didn't move to take it, he held it closer. "It's yours, and I want you to have it. For you and the baby."

Her curiosity was humming, and she slit open the envelope while he waited on the porch. When she saw what it contained, she stared at him in astonishment. "This is a cashier's check for an awful lot of money."

"Everything I took from our joint account, plus what I would've put in there after I left." Pausing, he swallowed and fixed her with a remorseful look. "Lindsay, I'm so sorry for what I did, leaving that way. I know it was wrong, and I hope you'll let me make it up to you."

She had to admit, that sounded intriguing. But she'd learned the hard way not to trust the smooth-talking man standing in front of her. "How?"

"It's freezing out here. Can I please come in?"

Since he'd just handed her more money than she'd had in nearly a year, Lindsay decided it would be all right to hear him out in a warmer spot. Stepping back, she let him in and tucked the precious envelope into a drawer in the hall table before facing him. "You've got five minutes, less if you make me mad. I'd suggest you choose your words carefully."

"Tough as ever, aren't you?" Chuckling, he pulled off his gloves and slipped them into his coat pocket. "I always liked that about you."

"You're down to four and a half minutes. Get to the point."

His dark eyes narrowed in obvious disapproval, but he quickly recovered. "All right, have it your way. Is this baby mine?"

His tactless question tripped every one of her childhood buttons, and she barely held back a scream. Furious beyond belief, she flung the heavy door open again. "Get out."

"I'm sorry," he backpedaled, holding up his hands in a calming gesture. "I just thought it was best to know for sure."

"I was never unfaithful to you when we were together. Can you say the same to me?" He didn't touch that one, and his evasion gave a little boost to her confidence. "That's a shame, really it is. It proves to me that I was right."

"About what?"

"You're not the kind of father I want for my daughter."

"It's a girl?"

His eyes went to her stomach, and she realized that she'd rested her hands protectively over her unborn child. She regretted giving him even that much information, but she couldn't go back and un-say it, so she kept going. "Yes. But you don't have to worry about us. We've gotten along just fine without you, and we'll keep on doing it after you leave."

"That's not what I want," he insisted. "I want us to be together, the way we should have been all along. I know I haven't handled this right, but I promise you I've changed. I'm a sales rep for a big pharmaceutical company now, and I'm making really good money. It won't be like it was before, scraping to get by all the time. I can take care of you and our daughter the way a man is supposed to do."

At one time, she'd wished over and over for him to come back and tell her just that. But now that she'd rediscovered her independence, she had no intention of giving it up. "That's not going to happen. You had your chance with me, and you blew it. You don't get another one. And your five minutes are up, so I'd appreciate it if you'd leave before I have to call the sheriff."

"I'm not going anywhere until we work this out."

He reached for her hands, and she pulled away to avoid his touch. Something stopped her momentum, and she looked back to find Brian standing behind her. He gently rested his hands on her shoulders, his normally warm blue eyes steely with anger.

"The lady asked you to leave," he said in a deadly calm voice. "I suggest you do what she says."

At first, Jeff didn't seem to recognize him. When

he did, he assessed Brian's grimy work clothes with a smug look. "Brian Calhoun. Still playing blacksmith?"

"You're trespassing on my grandmother's property. I'm gonna ask you one more time to leave."

Jeff took a threatening step toward him. "Or what?"

In one blur of motion, Brian stepped in front of Lindsay and folded his arms in an unmistakable warning. The two of them glared at each other, and she held her breath, wondering which of them would back down first. If they refused to break it up before things got physical, she wasn't sure what she'd be able to do.

Finally, she'd had enough of the macho display and put herself in between them. "Jeff, there's really no point in you being here. You need to go."

"We have to iron a few things out first," he insisted in a tone that told her he meant business. He gave Brian a haughty look. "In private."

"This is my grandmother's house," Brian reminded him curtly. "I'm not going anywhere."

"Oh, knock it off, you two," she scolded them, glowering from one to the other. "If you want to fight, take it outside."

Brian looked over his potential opponent with a cocky grin. "I don't think that'd end well for you."

"Try me."

She let out an exasperated breath. "Don't be stupid, guys. I was just kidding." Turning to her champion, she smiled. "Thanks for coming to my rescue, but I'll be fine."

"Yeah," he replied, drawing out the word as if he was coming up with a decent argument against her suggestion. "I'm starving, so I'm gonna go fix myself a snack."

He traded wary looks with Jeff, who shrugged. "Fine with me."

Relieved that his reasonable nature had prevented a potentially dangerous confrontation with her ex, Lindsay rewarded Brian with a quick peck on the cheek as he moved past her.

And then, a single breath later, everything changed.

Lindsay gasped, jerking away from him in a startled motion that sent Brian's heart into panic mode. "What's wrong?"

Pressing a hand to her side, she held up a finger for him to wait. Pain contorted her face, and she sagged, leaning against him for several long seconds. When she recovered a little, she looked up at him with terrified eyes. "I think my water just broke."

"You think?" Jeff demanded.

"I've never done this before," she shot back angrily. "So I'm not really sure, but that's what it felt like."

She doubled over again, and Brian helped her over to sit on one of the wide oak steps. Feeling completely helpless, he offered her a hand, and she proceeded to crush it in a grip that could've strangled a good-sized moose.

"Okay, that's good enough for me," he decided, unwilling to take any chances. "Let's get you to the hospital."

"I'm not due for two weeks," she protested breathlessly.

"I'm no expert, but I'm pretty sure Taylor decides when it's time to be born. It looks like she's gonna be impatient like her mama."

Saying the baby's name was a stroke of genius, he realized, as the fear in Lindsay's eyes gave way to a blend of love and determination. "You're right, we shouldn't take any chances."

"My truck's out front, so we'll get going and I'll call folks from the road."

"She'll be a lot more comfortable in my car," Jeff argued.

A few choice words came to mind, and Brian actually bit his tongue to keep them to himself. Fortunately, Lindsay settled the matter in her usual logical way.

"Brian knows the way, so I'll go with him. Jeff, you can follow us if you want, but you're not getting past the waiting room."

Satisfied, Brian watched Jeff trudge out to his fancy foreign sedan. After helping Lindsay into her coat, he paused for what he now realized was a for-real contraction, not the practice ones she'd experienced before. Trying to stay as calm as a guy could in this situation, he held her steady until she relaxed. Gazing down at this brave, strong-minded woman, he gave her a smile of encouragement. "Ready?"

"I hope so."

He managed to help her into his truck and get under way before the next contraction hit. They seemed to be coming pretty quickly, and he glanced at the dashboard clock each time she went into her breathing routine. He didn't have the first clue about how to deliver a baby, so he did the only thing he could.

Please Lord, he prayed silently. *Let us get to the hospital in time.*

While he followed the winding detour that led to the highway, he put his phone on speaker and called the hospital to let them know Lindsay was on her way.

When he called Holly, his very practical sister-in-law reacted just the way he'd expected.

"You hang in there, Lindsay," she ordered in the up-beat way that had enchanted Sam the first time they met. "I'm just a few minutes behind you."

"Will you say a prayer for us?" Lindsay asked, sounding more scared by the second.

"Already done."

With that assurance, she hung up, and Brian shut off his phone to save the battery. From what he'd read about childbirth in Lindsay's parenting books, he had a feeling they were all in for a very long day.

Waterford was a good half-hour trip, but he wasn't sure she'd last that long. Pushing the speed limit as much as he dared, he glanced over at his grim-faced passenger. "Doing okay?"

She nodded, but the tension in her back and shoulders told him otherwise. Hoping to distract her, he turned on the radio and kept up a fairly mindless stream of chatter all the way to the hospital.

When they arrived, the receptionist at the front door was taking down Lindsay's information when Jeff stormed in behind them. Clearly startled, she blinked up at him and asked, "May I help you?"

"I'm the father," he answered, a little out of breath from his run in from the parking lot.

The woman's eyes went to Brian. "I thought you were the father."

"It doesn't matter who the father is," Lindsay informed her through clenched teeth. "I'm the mother, and I'm pretty sure this baby's getting ready to be born right here in the lobby."

That got everyone's attention, and a wheelchair appeared from thin air to whisk her in the direction of the elevators.

As he was watching her go down the wide hallway, Brian felt a heavy hand on his shoulder.

"Thanks for your help," Jeff said in the smooth tone of a professional salesman. "We'll take it from here."

"I promised Lindsay I'd stay."

"Well, I'm here now, so that's really not necessary."

From down the hall, he heard a screech. "Brian!"

"That's my cue," he said, jogging to catch up with Lindsay. He wouldn't have minded the chance to get in a parting shot at Jeff, but right now his focus was on keeping the soon-to-be mother as calm as possible.

He'd anticipated leaving the delivery room once she was settled, but she had a death grip on his hand. Resigning himself to staying until Holly could get there, he searched his memory for what birthing coaches were supposed to do. "Want some ice chips?"

"Yes, but I don't want you to leave."

Brian couldn't manage both jobs at once, but an alternative came to mind, and he couldn't help grinning. "I'll send Jeff."

"Whatever," she muttered, arching her back as another contraction hit.

Brian had just sent Jeff on his errand when Holly left the elevator, all but running toward him. "How's it going?"

"Fast. I thought this kinda thing was supposed to take all day."

"Sometimes it does, sometimes it's quick. How's Lindsay doing?"

"Cranky," he replied honestly. "Terrified."

"That sounds about right." Opening the door, she asked, "Are you staying?"

He hadn't planned on it, counting on Holly's presence to be more than enough support to get Lindsay through her labor. But to his surprise, he heard himself say, "If she wants me to."

Holly rewarded his gesture with a bright smile. "You're a good guy, Brian. I'll go ask her."

Jeff came back just as Lindsay's unmistakable shriek settled the matter. "Brian!"

He almost said something to their unwelcome guest, but when Jeff's shoulders slumped in a defeated motion, Brian almost felt sorry for him. So instead of gloating, he kept his mouth shut and went back into Lindsay's room.

Unfortunately, it didn't take long for his expectation of a short labor to go out the window.

Chapter Ten

"Here you go, Lindsay," Holly cooed, handing her an impossibly small bundle wrapped in a soft pink blanket. "She's all yours."

Exhausted beyond words, from somewhere deep inside her, Lindsay found the strength to take Taylor in her arms. As soon as those blue-gray eyes squinted up at her, she was a goner.

Running a fingertip over the tiny chin, she marveled at the perfection of the little person she'd been waiting so long to meet. "I can't believe she's finally here."

"She's beautiful, just like her mama," Brian commented. Chuckling, he added, "And she's got a great set of lungs."

"Everything looks good, Lindsay," the nurse assured her, beaming as if this was the first child she'd helped to bring into the world instead of the latest of dozens. "You did a fantastic job."

"Thanks," Lindsay replied, dropping her head back against the pillows. "I've never been so tired in my life."

"Get used to it," the woman told her with a laugh. "You're a mom now, and that's part of the package."

She left, and after a quick hug, Holly followed after her. When they were gone, Lindsay smiled down at her daughter, still hardly able to comprehend what had gone on today. It had all happened so fast, she hadn't had a chance to let it soak in until now.

"I'm a mom now," she repeated softly, ticking the delicately upturned nose with her finger. "And you're my daughter. I guess that makes us a family."

"Of course it does," Brian said.

"But there's only two of us."

"Numbers don't mean much outside of those spreadsheets you beat me over the head with," he told her in that confident tone she'd come to rely on to bolster her spirits when they began to fall. "Love is what makes a family. As long as you've got that, everything else is just details."

"It's sweet of you to say that."

"But you don't believe me?"

"I'm not sure," she confided hesitantly. "I want to, but it's hard."

"Lindsay." When she looked up at him, his eyes twinkled with unmistakable affection. "You're nothing like your mother, and you won't make the same mistakes she did. You're gonna be a great mom."

"How can you be so sure?"

"Because I know you, and you'll do what's best for Taylor. Even when it might not be easy for you."

The nurse returned and very tactfully suggested to Brian that it was time for him to go. Grinning good-naturedly, he dropped a kiss on the baby's forehead.

"Taylor, it was cool to finally meet you." Turning to Lindsay, he paused as if he didn't quite know what to do. Then he leaned in and brushed a kiss over her cheek before murmuring, "Nice work, Holland. I'll see you around."

With that, he strolled from the cozy room as if he hadn't just spent most of his day with her whining and crushing his hand. She'd do something nice for him later, she vowed as she tugged the blanket closer around her sleeping daughter. Right now, she just wanted to admire the perfect little being that had made her way into the world.

"I'm already in love with her."

Startled by the sound of another voice, Lindsay looked up to find Jeff standing in the doorway, a huge bouquet of flowers in one hand and an enormous white teddy bear in the other. The stuffed animal had a pink satin ribbon around its neck and another around one fuzzy ear. Even though she wasn't thrilled about seeing him again so soon, Lindsay had to give him credit: he'd chosen the ideal birthday gift for Taylor.

"I thought you left hours ago," she chided him quietly to avoid waking the baby.

"I did," he confirmed as he continued to hang in the doorway. "I stayed in the waiting room, just like the nurse told me to. When I saw Brian leave, I decided to try seeing my girls. May I come in?"

The way he referred to them as "my" girls grated on her nerves, but Lindsay figured that if she said no, he'd only come back tomorrow and try again. And again, until the whole routine would become aggravating to her and confusing to the poor maternity ward nurses. "Fine, but only for a few minutes. Taylor needs her sleep, and I'm beyond exhausted."

"I can just imagine," he said, easing the door closed so it didn't make a sound. He sat in the bedside chair, angling his head to get a good look. "She's beautiful. Just like her mama," he added with an admiring look up at Lindsay.

His compliment echoed Brian's earlier one, and for a brief, insane moment, she felt herself smiling in response. Alarmed by how quickly he'd skirted her well-honed defenses, she called up a more appropriate scowl. "What do you want, Jeff?"

"To visit you and Taylor," he said in a wounded tone, as if he was surprised at being forced to explain his presence. "Why else would I hang around this hospital all day long? Did you know it's almost eight o'clock?"

That explained why she was so famished, Lindsay thought as her stomach rumbled impatiently. The doctor had commented on her "quick" labor, but it had actually taken nine hours. If that was a short labor, she hoped she never had to endure a long one.

"So," he went on in a tentative voice that was very unlike him. "How are you feeling, besides tired?"

"Fine."

"Good, because I have to discuss something with you."

"I'm not making any decisions about anything right now," she informed him curtly. "And for the record, I've done my research on parental rights. Since we're not married, you don't have a claim to anything where Taylor's concerned unless I agree to it."

"I'm well aware of that," he replied stiffly. Then, as if someone had flipped a switch, he gave her a softer, almost wistful look. "I'm also hoping that you'll give me the chance to make things right between us."

Before she could cut him down, he slid a velvet box out of the pocket of his coat. It opened with a little creak, revealing a lovely engagement ring that sparkled even in the dim lighting of her hospital room.

Taking it from the box, he fixed her with the adoring gaze she vaguely remembered from their earlier days together. "Lindsay, I know that in the past I made some horrible mistakes that ended up hurting you. I sincerely regret that, and I'd love nothing more than to make a family with you and Taylor. Will you marry me?"

Her jaw fell open in astonishment, and she honestly couldn't come up with anything to say. In her mind, she recognized that he'd pushed her most sensitive button, offering her the family she'd always longed for. Taylor began to stir, and as she looked down at her daughter, Lindsay's heart swelled with more love than she'd ever thought it was possible to experience.

Taylor deserved two parents, working together, nurturing her into the kind of strong, confident young woman who'd be able to succeed no matter what life threw at her. Having never known her own father, Lindsay yearned to give this child a more stable home life, so that she'd always know she was cherished, even if she messed up on occasion.

But was marrying Jeff the way to get that? Lindsay wondered. He seemed to be sincere about the changes he'd made, and from what she could see, he was making the most of his new career opportunity. Maybe once he had a family to support, he'd leave his irresponsible past behind for good and be the man they needed him to be.

And what if he didn't?

And what about Brian? The man who'd taken them both to his big, generous heart, and promised never to let them down?

Too worn-out to think clearly, she recognized that

she was in no condition to decide something this important. For herself, Lindsay wouldn't have worried. She'd been through a few failed relationships, and when things didn't work out, she scolded herself for being stupid and moved on.

But things were different now. It wasn't just about her anymore.

"I'm not sure," she hedged, feeling more drained by the second. "Can I think about it?"

"Absolutely," he agreed without hesitation, as if that was the response he'd been anticipating. Standing, he smiled down at her. "Take all the time you need. I'll be staying at the Waterford Inn, and here's my contact info."

He slipped a business card beneath the ring box, which he'd artfully left open so she could clearly see the beautiful ring. Then he leaned in to kiss Taylor's cheek but had the good sense not to do the same with Lindsay.

And with another smile, he was gone.

"Whoa," Brian commented when he poked his head into Lindsay's room the following afternoon. "Is that bear life-size?"

"Pretty much," she replied with a laugh. "But she's very friendly. Come on in."

The gigantic bouquet of pink roses sitting on the windowsill dwarfed his handful of wildflowers, and he felt awkward putting his simple ceramic vase next to the crystal one. He'd never been one to compare himself to other guys, but for some reason, this time he felt as if he didn't quite measure up. It didn't help that he'd never liked Jeff Mortensen. But he didn't want to risk making a comment that would come across as petty to her, so he decided to just pretend the flowers weren't there.

Sitting in the only chair, he grinned over at the mother and daughter cuddled together. "So, how're you girls doing today?"

"Just fine. The nurse took Taylor to the nursery for part of the night so I could get some sleep. I feel like a brand-new person."

She looked happier than he'd seen her since she first arrived in town, but Brian didn't know how to say that without making it sound like an insult, so he kept the observation to himself. Glancing over at the other flowers and balloon bouquets that occupied the rolling table, he was pleased to see how many people had sent the new mother something to celebrate Taylor's arrival. Among the vases and baby-themed trinkets, he noticed something nestled in among the others that was unmistakable.

Picking up the velvet box, he admired the glittering diamonds set around the ring. He felt a pang of regret that he wasn't in a position to make a grand gesture like that for her. "Something you wanna tell me, Holland?"

"Jeff was here," she said simply, looking down at the sleeping baby in her arms in an obvious attempt to avoid his eyes.

"And?"

Lindsay gave him a "give me a break" kind of look. "What do you think?"

"I think he asked you to marry him. You said 'maybe' and he left the ring to tempt you into making it a yes."

"That's pretty much how it happened," she allowed, sighing at the beautiful enticement he'd left behind for her. "I'm just not sure what to do."

"Seriously?" Floored by her revelation, Brian didn't even bother trying to hold back his opinion. "After what he did to you? To Taylor? He left you with no car, no money and started a new life somewhere else."

"When he found out about Taylor, he came back," she pointed out in a meek tone that sounded nothing like the woman he'd been getting to know. "He returned all the money, and he says he wants to take care of us."

"For how long?" Brian demanded, his temper quickly reaching the boiling point. "When things get tough, the guy has a nasty habit of taking off and letting someone else clean up after him. How long do you think he'll last when it dawns on him that he's responsible for two other people?"

"He's Taylor's father," Lindsay reminded him sternly. "I want her to at least have a chance at the kind of family I never had."

Now it made sense, Brian realized. Having missed out on the love and stability of a supportive family, more than once Lindsay had told him how much she appreciated being included in the Calhouns' circle. That sense of belonging was something he'd always taken for granted, but he could understand how important it would be to someone who'd never had that in their life.

So rather than browbeat Lindsay with facts, he opted for a more personal approach. "Do you really believe Jeff can give her that?"

"I'm not sure," she admitted, resting her head back against the pile of pillows. Giving him a wistful look, she sent him a half-hearted smile. "That's why I didn't say yes. But part of me thinks I should give him the opportunity to prove that he's changed."

In her hesitation, Brian heard a sliver of an opening. "What about the other part?"

She shrugged as if it didn't matter all that much, and his heart plunged to the floor. Lindsay was a practical woman, and if her brain was telling her that marrying Jeff was a good idea, it wasn't likely that anyone—not even him—could talk her out of it.

Even though he feared that it would be the biggest mistake of her life, he recognized that the decision was hers to make. So, he stood and set the ring back in its spot. Forcing a smile he didn't really feel, he said, "I'll let you two get some sleep. If you need anything, you know how to reach me."

"Thanks, Brian. I really am grateful for everything you've done for us."

To his ears, that sounded a lot like an emotional farewell, and he kept his smile frozen in place until he left her room. Out in the hallway, he finally let it drop as he walked through the cheery maternity wing to the elevator. A few of the people he saw on his way out gave him long, curious looks, but he didn't care. His day had taken a real nosedive, and as he racked his brain for a solution, he realized that there was absolutely nothing he could do about it.

Back at the forge, he found a note on the door from Sam.

Riley and I went to the hardware store. Back soon.

That was actually a good thing, Brian thought as he unlocked the door and went inside. He wasn't in the mood for conversation right now. Stopping in the open lobby, he looked to his left at the project that he'd been working on for days.

The formerly shoe-box-sized office area was much

bigger now, enclosed by half walls with a Dutch door that could be closed and still allow visitors to see inside. The makeshift workspace had tripled in size, complete with a lightly used suite of oak furniture and the burgundy leather executive's desk chair that Lindsay had admired and bookmarked on her laptop weeks ago. Off to the side was a brightly painted half bath, and on the other was another Dutch door that led to a small room outfitted with a crib, changing table and padded rocking chair. An interior designer, Holly had helped him plan and stock the nursery, and even a bachelor like him could appreciate the bright, cheerful space.

Once he and Sam had finished the major structural improvements to the building, Brian had been working every evening on the new area, motivated by the idea of surprising Lindsay with it when she came back to work after her maternity leave. Intended as a gift to her and Taylor, now it seemed like a colossal waste of time. Reality hit him like a truck, and he sank into the rocking chair, wishing he'd never started this nonsense in the first place.

"Whatcha doin'?" Sam asked as he strolled in, a box of nails under one arm and Riley trotting at his heels.

"Nothing." His big brother came back with a doubtful look, and when Riley sat beside him, wrinkling his forehead in canine agreement, Brian had to laugh. "Okay, I'm feeling like an idiot for jumping the gun on this. I should've asked Lindsay first."

"She doesn't like it?"

"She doesn't even know about it."

"You just lost me," Sam said, leaning against the doorjamb with a confused expression. "Everything was fine when you left for Waterford. Why don't you back up and start at the beginning?"

So Brian told him the whole maddening story. When he was finished, he gave his levelheaded older brother a grim look. "Whatta you think?"

"I don't know Lindsay that well, so I couldn't say what's going through her head. It sounds to me like you think she's gonna say yes to this guy."

"And leave Liberty Creek," Brian added glumly, motioning around the cozy room. "Meaning this was all for nothing."

"So we'll repaint it and make it into a storage room. The real problem is how you'd feel about losing Lindsay." Sam gave him a knowing look. "Judging by your attitude, you'd miss her."

"Sure I would. She keeps this place running, and without her I would've gone out of business by now."

"And?"

Brian had an idea where this was headed, and he glared back. "And what?"

"I get that you like working with her, but anyone who has eyes can see there's more to it than that."

"You're outta your mind," Brian scoffed. "The woman drives me to the edge of my sanity on a regular basis, and we fight constantly. But she keeps the office and finances on track, and we make a good team. It's not like I can run an ad in the paper or online and replace her, y'know. I tried that before and got nowhere."

Sam assessed him with a pensive look, and Brian braced himself for more personal questions he didn't want to answer. Instead, Sam said, "Then I guess you'll have to wait and see what she does. She might surprise you."

She'd done that constantly since the day he met her at seventeen, so it was conceivable that she'd do it again. "You really think so?"

"This is a big decision for her to make, and it affects her daughter, too. I think your best approach is to hang back and be patient, let her make up her mind without pressuring her. And have a little faith. Things will work out the way they're meant to."

Coming from his towering older brother, the philosophical comment made Brian grin. "They did for you, didn't they?"

"Better than I ever could've hoped for. God brought Lindsay here for a reason, and whether she leaves or stays, it's because that's what He intended from the start."

"Yeah, I guess you're right," Brian agreed, sighing as he got to his feet. "I just wish I could skip to the end and see how this all turns out."

"Life would be pretty boring if we could do that. For now, let's get back to work and finish off this project. Maybe things will fall your way and you'll end up needing it, after all."

Lindsay had never been so happy to be anywhere.

Pulling into Ellie's driveway felt more like coming home than she'd imagined it would, with the large house nestled in its snowy yard and smoke lazily drifting from the chimney. Every paved surface had been shoveled clear, and the slight haze on top made it obvious someone had spread enough salt to keep them from slushing over again.

When she mentioned all the work someone had done,

her adoptive grandmother smiled. "Brian was here earlier, making sure everything was safe for you and Taylor."

Lindsay couldn't help noticing that he wasn't here now, though. Or that he hadn't offered to drive her home from the hospital. In fact, since his last awkward visit to her hospital room, she hadn't heard a word from him. After spending so much time with him recently, his absence was aggravating, to say the least. "So, I'm guessing he's pretty busy."

"And then some. Now, do you want me to help with the car seat, or have you got it figured out?"

"I've got it."

That was a stretch, but Lindsay knew that she'd have to get the hang of it sooner or later. Then again, until she actually bought a car, the plush safety seat wouldn't get much use. That was the old, negative Lindsay talking, she scolded herself, pushing the grumbling away while she focused on releasing the seat from its base. To her relief, it came free, and she followed Ellie into the house.

Taylor's eyes slitted open, and she squinted at the unfamiliar surroundings. She couldn't see very far yet, but she obviously recognized that she'd been moved, and Lindsay wondered what the infant thought of the change. Apparently, not much, because her eyes drifted closed again without her making so much as a peep. Lindsay hated to ruin that, but she knew that leaving the baby in her little winter cocoon wasn't the right thing to do, either.

So she braced herself for some fussing and slipped Taylor out of her layers as gently as possible. Fortunately, the protest was brief, and she snuggled against

Lindsay, resting her cheek on her shoulder with a contented sigh.

"Such a precious little thing," Ellie murmured, running a practiced hand over Taylor's silky hair. "I hope you're planning to stay here awhile, because I'd really love having a baby in the house again."

Lindsay wasn't sure what her long-term plans were, but she wasn't in a hurry to change anything right now. She couldn't imagine too many people who'd be eager to open their home to an inexperienced single mom and a possibly noisy infant, and her heart filled with gratitude for this generous woman who'd done just that. "That's very gracious of you, and I really appreciate it. You have no idea how much your support means to me. The whole family has been awesome."

"The family?" Ellie echoed with a knowing look. "Why do I get the feeling you're doing your best not to refer to anyone in particular?"

"That's not true." That got her a raised eyebrow, and she couldn't help laughing. "Okay, you got me. I was talking about Brian. He's been so great through all this, I was kind of expecting him to drive us home, or at least be here to greet us."

"I think he wanted to."

Lindsay sensed that there was something weird going on, and she nudged. "But?"

Ellie hesitated, as if she was debating whether or not she should get involved in her very stubborn grandson's personal business. Finally, she said, "I'm not sure he knows where the two of you stand. With each other," she added in an obvious attempt to clarify things.

"We're friends," Lindsay answered immediately, baffled by the need to discuss the matter at all. "And in spite of our differences, we work well together. I didn't realize anyone was confused about that."

Ellie didn't say anything, and the mellow knock of the grandfather clock's pendulum echoed in the silence. Given time to reflect, it dawned on Lindsay what Ellie was trying very hard not to tell her. "Do you think Brian's confused about what we are?"

"Possibly," she admitted with a delicate shrug. "I've never seen him go to this much trouble for the women he dates."

"But we're not dating," Lindsay protested. That got her a gentle smile, and because she was holding a sleeping Taylor, she did a mental forehead slap. "Which is your point, that he's been putting in all that time and effort to impress me. Why didn't you just say so?"

"It's none of my business, dear," Ellie reminded her primly, passing by on her way into the kitchen. "You two aren't teenagers anymore, and you're smart enough to work this out for yourselves."

Food for thought, Lindsay mused as she began to head upstairs to put Taylor in her pretty wicker bassinet. Someone knocked on the front door, and she turned back. "I'll get it, Ellie!"

"Thank you!"

Lindsay opened the heavy door to find Jeff standing on the brick porch, wearing an anxious look that she'd never seen on him. Normally self-assured to the point of arrogance, now he looked as if he expected to be unceremoniously tossed out into the snow.

"Hi, Lindsay," he said in a voice that sounded almost humble. "May I come in?"

She wasn't exactly in the mood for company, but she couldn't come up with a decent reason to refuse him, so she stepped back to let him in. "But not for long. Us girls need a nap."

"I understand." The tension left his face as he gazed down at Taylor, and he bent down to kiss her forehead in the kind of loving gesture that reminded Lindsay of why she'd fallen for him all those years ago. Lifting his gaze to Lindsay, he asked, "Is it all right with you if I hold her?"

Reflexively, Lindsay pulled the baby closer. Then reason kicked in to remind her that Jeff was the child's father, and he had a right to hold her. "Okay."

The handoff was a bit awkward, but when he finally had her, he relaxed enough to smile at her and then Lindsay. "She's the second-prettiest girl I've ever met."

It was the kind of thing he used to say, when she was mad at him for something he'd done—or hadn't done—and was seeking to get back on her good side. But this time, for some reason she didn't feel the same warm, fuzzy response to his attention. She wasn't angry, either, and she searched her mind for a way to define what was going on. After a few moments, she realized what it was.

Nothing.

She no longer hated him, but she didn't love him anymore, either. Somewhere over the past several months, she'd regained enough of her dignity to realize that not only did she not need Jeff anymore, she didn't even want him. She was perfectly capable of taking care of herself and her daughter on her own, and knowing that made her feel stronger than she ever had in her life.

Taylor began to squirm, and Jeff quickly handed her back. When she was quiet again, he cleared his throat before asking, "So, have you had a chance to think about what we discussed the other day?"

The stilted phrasing reminded her of a businessman addressing a client, and she actually felt a sting of remorse for keeping him in the dark for so long. Still holding Taylor, she went to her overnight bag and took the velvet box from its place in the outside pocket. She wasn't sure what to say, so she simply held it out to him.

Looking from her hand to her face, he shook his head. "I don't understand. We're Taylor's parents. We should get married and make a family for her."

In that moment, Lindsay understood why she'd been so hesitant to commit to marrying him. He didn't necessarily want her back, but he was a good enough man to want to be Taylor's father. Stalling while she searched for a way to explain it, she summoned all the patience she had for what would no doubt be a difficult conversation.

"I appreciate that you want to be part of Taylor's life," she began, adding a smile that she hoped would soften the blow of her words. "But just being legally bound together isn't enough. Do you still love me?"

His eyes slid away from hers for a brief moment, before coming back with a determined stare. "Yes."

"Are you saying that because it's true, or because you think that's what I want to hear?"

"There's no one else, Lindsay."

That wasn't quite the declaration of undying devotion that she was after, but she didn't see the point in badgering him into admitting his honest feelings for her. Instead, she decided to do the gracious thing and let him off the hook. "Love is what makes a family, and I don't want us rushing into something we'll all regret later. Believe me, when parents split up, it's the kids who suffer the most. Taylor deserves better than that."

"But I'm her father," Jeff protested in a desperate tone that told her just how much this meant to him.

"That won't change," she promised him. "Your name is on her birth certificate, and we'll work out some kind of legal arrangement to give you time with her. I want her to know you, but we don't have to be married so you can have a relationship with your daughter. It won't be easy, but lots of people make it work. I'm sure we can, too."

He didn't respond at first, and the crestfallen look on his face made her feel awful. Still, she knew in her heart that this was the right decision for all of them. She no longer loved him, and she still had her misgivings about trusting him to keep a life-altering commitment like this. While on the surface marrying him might appear to make her life easier, it was the wrong thing to do.

"I have one question," he finally said. When she nodded for him to go on, he asked, "Does Brian Calhoun have anything to do with this?"

"Not a bit," she assured him, shaking her head to emphasize her point. "This is my choice to make, and I honestly believe that this is what's best for Taylor and me. When you have some time to think about it, I hope you'll agree that it's best for you, too."

"I won't ever see it that way." She didn't contradict him, and he relented with a sigh. "So that's it, then? This is really what you want?"

"Yes. Next time you're coming to the area on business, give me a few days' notice. I'll arrange for us to sit down with a lawyer and put together some kind of visitation agreement we can both live with."

"All right. I'd also like to have him add a section for me to help out financially."

She narrowed her eyes warily. "Is this your way of trying to change my mind about your proposal?"

"No. You made your decision, and I promise to respect it. But Taylor's my daughter, and even though we won't be together, I want to be as much of a father to her as I can."

Lindsay had been burned by him in the past, so she was leery of putting too much faith in him now. Still, Brian had given her a second chance and it had worked out well. Maybe she and Jeff could make peace with each other, too. "Thank you. I'll pass that along to the lawyer."

"I appreciate you doing that. I have a client meeting west of here tomorrow morning, and then I'll be heading back to New Haven in the afternoon. Is it all right if I stop by on my way back to Connecticut to say goodbye to Taylor?"

"Of course. If you'll give me a heads-up, I'll make sure she's awake when you come by."

"I'll do that."

He stepped forward, as if he meant to lean in for a kiss, but abruptly stopped. Pulling away, he gave her a self-conscious grimace and instead rested his hand on her shoulder. "I'll see you tomorrow."

"We'll be here," she assured him, opening the door to let him out.

After he'd driven away, Ellie met her in the foyer with the cordless phone. "It's Brian. Something about the printer not working."

It was the first time he'd contacted her in days, and Lindsay was more than a little surprised to hear from her wayward boss. Taking the phone, she decided to play it cool, even though her heart was hammering in her chest. "What's up?"

"This thing is jammed, and I went through the whole troubleshooting list you gave me. I even unplugged and restarted it, but no dice. I really need it, so I was hoping you had another idea."

"Not really. I'd have to see it to know why it's doing what it's doing."

He grumbled something, and she swallowed a laugh. To her knowledge, he'd always been good at everything he tried, so it was amusing to hear the self-assured blacksmith grousing like a normal human being.

"Hang on a sec." Resting the receiver against her shoulder, she asked, "Ellie, would you mind watching Taylor while I run over to the forge?"

"Of course not, dear. Take my car if you want."

Lindsay thanked her, then got back to Brian. "Taylor's sound asleep, so I'll be right over. Don't touch anything else."

"Awesome," he said heartily, then quickly hung up.

Taylor never moved when Lindsay settled her into her little bed, and she sneaked out of the room as silently as she could manage. It took about two minutes to get to the ironworks, and when Lindsay went through the newly stained front door, she came to a dead stop in the middle of the lobby. The rustic decor was gone, replaced by a set of furniture that was obviously used but all matched. A half wall now enclosed the office area, with a Dutch door in the center that allowed access and a clear view of whoever might be coming in.

Walking through the bright, welcoming space, she opened the door and went into a proper office, complete with an L-shaped desk and bookcases all made of honey oak. Behind the desk sat Brian, scowling at the printer as if he honestly believed that would get him anywhere.

"Glaring at it won't help," she teased as she joined him inside.

He gave her a mournful look that told her he'd been wrestling with the troublesome piece of equipment for far too long before asking for her help. "I hate to bug you, but I'm totally stumped."

Angling her head, she asked, "Is that the chair I liked?"

"Yeah. I found it at the office supply depot where Gran got hers."

"That was the most expensive one we looked at," she scolded him mildly. Though it was hard to be angry at someone who'd shelled out money he didn't have in an attempt to make her happy. "You shouldn't have spent that much on a chair."

Standing, he swiveled it on a smooth pivot, as if to remind her of why she'd admired it in the first place. "It's the floor model, so they gave me a discount."

It was a sweet thing to do, so she decided to let the matter drop. In the back corner of the office, she noticed another Dutch door and strolled over to see what lay beyond it. When she saw the cozy nursery, she couldn't believe that he'd gone to so much effort to make her workspace more comfortable for her. Blinking back tears, she turned to him in astonishment. "Is this why I haven't heard from you since Taylor was born?"

"Partly."

"I can't believe you did all this. For all you knew, I'd be leaving town with Jeff."

Doubt flickered in his eyes, and his jaw tensed in obvious frustration. "Are you?"

"No, but you didn't know that. I didn't even know until this morning." To be truthful, she'd been alternating between "yes" and "no" right up until Jeff had appeared on Ellie's front porch.

Relief chased away the doubt in Brian's eyes, and a maddening smirk lifted the corner of his mouth. "So, seeing him again didn't make you want to jump for joy?"

"Not exactly," she admitted, allowing herself a little grin. "But depositing that cashier's check sure did."

"I'm glad he did that. I guess even a self-centered weasel can show some backbone once in a while."

"I'm not complaining."

"Speaking of money, I heard from Rick Marshall this morning," he announced.

"And?"

"The bank is satisfied that Liberty Creek Forge won't go belly-up in a month," he replied proudly. "Rick sent me a copy of the report he submitted, including a line about how the cost of a loan to a small business like this one is small compared to the value the forge has to the community."

"That must have made you feel pretty awesome."

"I didn't hate it, that's for sure. To top it off, he ordered one of those hanging pot racks for his kitchen. Said he's been looking for something like that but couldn't find one he liked until he saw these."

"That's fabulous. Congratulations." Glancing around the office, she couldn't help laughing at the mess. "However, this place is one step short of being declared a disaster zone. What on earth have you been doing?"

"I've just been piling everything where there's room for it. That winery order's been keeping me busy, on top of the others that keep rolling in. That's why I need the printer. The delivery guy taking those wine racks out is on his way, and I have to get the shipping labels on the boxes before he gets here."

His explanation sounded reasonable, but she got the impression that something else was going on with him. Now that she'd had the chance to really look at him, he looked beyond exhausted. But she suspected that it was more than fatigue dragging down that chiseled jaw. Hope sparked inside her, but she firmly tamped it down before it got out of control and left her disappointed. "Brian, what's going on?"

"Nothing. Why?"

"I live with your grandmother, remember? You came over to shovel the walks but left before we got home, like you're avoiding me." Folding her arms, she nailed him with her most direct stare. "That's not like you. What gives?"

His gaze slid away from her, as if he was trying desperately to hide something from her. "Wasn't sure you'd wanna see me."

"Since when?" He shrugged, and when he continued evading her eyes, she began to get a glimmer of what was bothering him. "Is it possible that you mean you didn't want to see me?"

Another shrug, but this time his eyes met hers in a hopeful look. "Can I ask you something?"

"Sure."

"Why'd you turn down Jeff's proposal?"

She explained her reasons, and he nodded as if he understood perfectly. Which was pretty amazing to her, since she didn't quite comprehend them herself. It was more of a listen-to-your-heart thing, and she was stunned that anyone other than her could follow it.

"So," Brian went on in a pensive tone, "you wanna be on your own."

"For now," she replied, taking a few tentative steps toward him. He didn't back away, and she took that as a good sign. "My life is very different now, and I've got a lot of adjustments to make. Mostly, I need to focus on Taylor and my job."

"I get that," he said, closing the remaining distance between them so they were within arm's reach of each other. "When you don't have so much on your plate, what then?"

"I suppose I'll figure that out when I get there."

Reaching out, he gently traced the curve of her cheek with his finger. "Would you be against having a little distraction once in a while?"

"What did you have in mind?"

"Dinner sometime. Maybe a movie that hasn't been on TV yet."

The twinkle she'd missed was shining in those deep blue eyes, and she couldn't suppress a smile. "Then I suppose that would depend on who was doing the distracting."

"What if it was me?"

In answer, she reached up to draw his face to hers for a kiss. When she started to pull back, he wrapped his arms around her and held her there, deepening the kiss into one that sent a warm current through her entire body.

When he released her, she gazed up at this wonderful man who'd come to mean so much more to her than she ever could have imagined.

"I think I could get my head around that."

Epilogue

"Man, am I glad that's over," Brian commented, rubbing his shoulder as he stood in the doorway of Lindsay's office. "I love having tourists in here, but doing three demonstrations in one day is tough on the old arm."

It was mid-May, and just as everyone had hoped, the mild weather had brought visitors into this part of New Hampshire by the dozens. Eager to experience the natural beauty of the area, many of them stopped by the freshly painted bridge to read the plaque that detailed its charming, homespun history. On the other side stood the intriguing Liberty Creek Forge, and they were more than happy to come in for the kind of living history lesson Brian had planned all along.

"This might help," she said, spinning her laptop so he could look over the pony wall and get a glimpse of the day's receipts. When his mouth fell open in a shocked O, she laughed. "Several of your guests had been in town before, and they mentioned how pretty the new bridge is. They used to wonder what was in this building, and they were thrilled to get a chance to take a trip back in time with a blacksmith descended from the original founders."

Brian gave her a knowing look. "You're using that line on the website, aren't you?"

"As soon as I get Taylor home and fed. She always takes a nap after dinner, so I should have just enough quiet time to make some online edits."

As if she'd understood what they were talking about, Taylor began kicking in her bouncy seat, gurgling her opinion of their itinerary. Riley was stretched out on a braided rug beside her, which was his customary post whenever the baby was nearby. Perking up in a canine version of Taylor's reaction, he cocked his head in obvious interest.

"Sounds like a plan," Brian agreed. Leaning on the low wall, he gave her one of those irresistible crooked grins. "It's still pretty nice outside. What do you say we knock off early and I'll walk you ladies home?"

Riley yipped, and his owner laughed. "Yes, you can come, too. But you've gotta be quiet. Last time we went over there, you got the neighbor's coonhound howling, and folks didn't appreciate it."

The multicolored shepherd whined a sort of apology, and Lindsay couldn't help laughing while she closed down her computer. "Now you've made him feel bad. Dogs bark at each other. If people don't like that, they should stick to cats."

"I'm with you there." Opening the Dutch door, he slung the diaper bag over his shoulder as if it was the most natural thing in the world for him to do.

"You know, that should look ridiculous," Lindsay teased as she packed up her laptop and lifted Taylor from her seat. "But you make it work somehow."

"I'm a modern guy," he protested in a wounded tone that was betrayed by the humor twinkling in his eyes. "When there's a job to do, I roll up my sleeves and get it done. Taylor likes that about me."

Pausing in the middle of the lobby, Lindsay smiled and craned her neck to peck him on the cheek. "So do I."

The grin warmed to something much more personal, and she suspected that if he hadn't been playing pack mule, it would have taken them a while to leave the forge. Their experiments in "distraction" had been infrequent but very successful, and she was enjoying the way he managed to defer to her and pamper her at the same time.

"So, is Jeff still coming this weekend?" he asked in a casual way that did nothing to hide his lingering mistrust of her ex.

"Yes, but I'll be around, just in case. We agreed that for now, he'll visit Taylor at home so she can stay on her schedule."

"I'm kinda surprised he went for that."

"I didn't give him an option," Lindsay told him. "Legally, he doesn't have any rights beyond what I give him, so it's my way or nothing."

Brian flashed her an approving grin. "Good for you."

Once outside, he locked the door to the forge and rested his arm lightly around her shoulders for the stroll through town to Ellie's house. It hadn't escaped her that since she and Brian had officially been together, no one dared to look askance at her. She knew it was more because they were afraid of his temper than out of respect for her, but she was grateful for his unwavering commitment to being her knight in shining armor. She was hardly a damsel in distress, but it was still nice to know he had her back.

Riley came from behind them, leading the way for a few yards, then circling behind them before trotting back to the front. The dog seemed as happy as anyone that the long-anticipated spring had finally arrived.

"He's really filled out since you took him in," Lindsay commented. "And he's a big hit with people visiting the forge. It's like you've always had him."

"If I could just get him to sleep at the foot of the bed instead of crammed up next to me," Brian replied with a chuckle. "It'd nice to be able to stretch out again."

Several people were out enjoying a walk in the late-afternoon sunshine, and the sound of some eager beaver's lawn mower rumbled from somewhere nearby. The trees and shrubs surrounding the square were beginning to put out buds, and there was a group of kids playing catch while their friends set up bases for an impromptu game of baseball. The door of the bakery stood open, letting out the sounds of Duke Ellington and the smell of something that made Riley start sniffing the air.

"Don't even think about it, dude," Brian warned him sternly. "The last time you went in there, Gran's customers had a fit. Don't make me go and buy a leash."

"He actually ran into the bakery?"

"Yeah. Hard to blame him, though, considering how good everything smells."

Lindsay saw his point, and she was impressed that the dog was able to ignore the temptation and continue walking toward the other end of Main Street. When they got to Ellie's, Lindsay got the mail and went ahead to open the front door and hold it open for Brian.

Inside, Taylor let out a stream of totally adorable

baby sounds that made it clear she realized they were home for the day.

"Someone's happy," Brian said, leaning in to rub noses with her. "That's how I always feel when I come here, too."

Lindsay caught sight of a large envelope from Waterford University and took a deep breath to steady her suddenly racing heart. "Brian, could you take Taylor so I can open this?"

"Sure."

In an easy motion, he took the baby into his arms. Taylor stared up at him in unabashed adoration, patting his cheek with a tiny hand before cuddling against his shoulder in an unmistakable show of trust. Lindsay frequently did that herself, and she knew just how reassuring it was to have him there, day in and day out. Sometimes she didn't even need the comforting, but he offered it all the same, allowing her the opportunity to either take it or stand on her own.

Having that kind of calm, steady influence in her life still amazed her sometimes. That he offered the same to her daughter was almost more than she could believe.

Her hands were shaking, but she managed to open the envelope and pull out the top sheet of parchment. Tears of joy flooded her eyes, and she read out loud. "'Dear Lindsay, it gives me great pleasure to welcome you to the psychology department of Waterford University. We look forward to seeing you in the fall.'"

"That's awesome!" Brian approved, rewarding her with a kiss before bouncing Taylor gently. "Mommy's gonna be a college student. Isn't that cool?"

Taylor clearly understood that he was asking her a

question, and she responded in some sweet nonsense that made them both laugh.

"I can't believe it," Lindsay said, staring at the letter that had changed her life in a matter of seconds.

"I can. I always knew you could do anything. You just had to want it bad enough."

He was being so great, she thought. But he must be wondering how this would affect his business. Eager to reassure him, she told him, "They have a lot of online and night classes available. I'll put together a schedule that won't interfere with my job at the forge."

"Your hours can be as flexible as you need them to be. Pick the courses you want, and we'll manage the business around them."

"You're sure?"

"Of course, I am," he answered, making it sound like a no-brainer. "Wouldn't have said it otherwise."

"That would be fabulous, Brian. Thank you."

"No problem. Why don't you go warm up Taylor's bottle?" he suggested, as if sensing that Lindsay could use a minute to herself. "We'll be in the living room soaking up the sun."

Grateful for the reprieve, Lindsay followed his suggestion and then joined them. Taking the baby who was the absolute joy of her life, she settled down to feed her while she caught Brian up on the other big news she'd gotten that day.

"I heard from that winery in Vermont, and their event was a huge success. There was a married couple there who asked where they got their racking, so she gave them the forge's contact information. She said they wanted it for displays and seemed very interested, so we should be hearing from them soon."

"What kind of business do they have?"

"Pottery, ceramics, that sort of thing," Lindsay answered, pausing when she realized that Taylor had drifted off. Lifting the sleeping baby to her shoulder, she covered her with one of Ellie's handmade afghans. "I'll just run her upstairs, if you don't mind waiting."

"Not a bit."

Leaning back in the wing chair, he folded his hands over his stomach and stretched his long legs out in the kind of pose that said he wasn't in a hurry to go anywhere. The always alert Riley followed her up to her room, sitting patiently while she settled Taylor into her bassinet and switched on the baby monitor. Taking the receiver with her, she walked back downstairs and was surprised to find the living room empty.

The front door was open, and on the other side of the screen she saw Brian sitting on the front steps, elbows resting on his bent knees while he looked out into the yard. Rugged and strong, he'd proven over and over that he was the kind of guy even a jaded girl like her could depend on. A rush of emotions surged up inside her, and for the thousandth time she wondered what she possibly could have done to deserve him.

Pushing the screen open, she let Riley out before setting the monitor down and joining Brian on the steps. Leaning her cheek against his arm, she sighed. "This is nice."

"Yeah," he agreed, lifting his arm to put it around her. "Makes up for all those eighteen-hour days I had at the beginning."

"Ugh, I remember those. I used to wonder how you managed to stay so positive all the time."

"No sense in being a pessimist," he reasoned calmly.

"If things get bad, you dig in and fix 'em. Worrying about what might or might not happen is a waste of energy."

Lindsay wished she could be that upbeat. "I'm more optimistic than I used to be, but I'm still a worrier."

"You're a mom. Worrying is part of the territory."

"I guess when you love someone, that's just how it works."

"I guess so." He was quiet for a few moments, then pulled away slightly to look down at her. When she met his eyes, she saw something in them that was so rare, she could count the times she'd noticed it on one hand. Uncertainty. "Did you want to say something else?"

He didn't answer at first, but the darkening blue in his eyes clued her in that something important was going on. To her immense relief, he gave her the warm smile she'd always treasured. "You may not want to hear this right now, but I love you, Lindsay. The honest truth is, I never stopped."

From nowhere, tears sprang into her eyes, and she blinked furiously to keep them in check. Returning that smile was the easiest thing she'd ever done, and she was only too happy to reassure him. "I love you, too. I think I always did, but I didn't realize it because I was too busy being stupid."

That got her a wry smirk. "So loving me is smart?"

"The smartest thing I've ever done."

She followed up her confession with a long kiss filled with gratitude for this man who'd never let her down, even when she'd given him all kinds of reasons to turn his back and walk away. Resting her hand on his cheek, she said, "Thank you for not giving up on me."

"Anytime. Y'know, I've been curious about something."

"What's that?"

Leaning to the side, he fished something from the pocket of his jeans and held it out in front of her. There, sparkling in the late-afternoon sunshine, was an antique diamond ring. Sliding it onto her finger, he gazed down at her with the most serious expression she'd ever seen on him. "Will you marry me?"

Stunned beyond words, she stared at the beautiful ring, trying to comprehend what had just happened. Designed with precise points and delicate scrolls, the setting reminded her of a piece of jewelry she'd seen before.

When it hit her, she sat upright and stared at him in amazement. "This looks like my watch."

"It is like your watch. They go together, like us."

The implication of what he'd done dawned on her, and she stared at him in amazement. "You bought this for me at that antique show you took me to six years ago?"

"Yeah. I went back for it later."

"And held on to it for six years, even after I left," she continued, still unable to believe it. "Why?"

"Lost the receipt." Her chiding look made him laugh. "Okay, you got me. I guess part of me hoped you'd come back, and we'd have another chance to get it right."

"That's crazy," she announced, easing the insult with a kiss. "And the most romantic thing I've ever heard."

"I'm gonna go out on a limb here," he teased, "and take that as a yes."

"Good, because that's how I meant it."

"You know you drive me nuts, right?"

"Till death do us part, Calhoun," she reminded him playfully, cuddling against him while she held out her hand to admire her ring.

Taking her hand in his, he brushed his lips over the back and smiled. "That's what I'm counting on."

* * * * *

*If you loved this tale of sweet romance,
pick up the first book
in the* LIBERTY CREEK *series
from author Mia Ross:*

MENDING THE WIDOW'S HEART

*And check out these other stories
from Mia Ross's previous miniseries,*
OAKS CROSSING:

*HER SMALL-TOWN COWBOY
RESCUED BY THE FARMER
HOMETOWN HOLIDAY REUNION
FALLING FOR THE SINGLE MOM*

Available now from Love Inspired!

Find more great reads at www.LoveInspired.com.

Dear Reader,

I hope you enjoyed your visit to snowy Liberty Creek!

I was watching one of my favorite home improvement shows one day, and there was a guest star who ran a custom metalworking shop. He made that cold, impersonal medium into beautiful works of art, and an idea started forming in my head. I remembered going to a local living history museum and a Renaissance festival and being fascinated by the blacksmiths and how the tools of their trade hadn't changed much in the three hundred years separating their eras. From there, Brian Calhoun's vintage forge and the challenges it would face operating in this century came to life for me, and the research was some of the most interesting I've ever done.

But as good a metalsmith as he was, he needed some help. Lindsay Holland walked onto the stage of this charming little town, and I liked her right away. Sassy, smart and independent, she's the kind of woman I admire: one who takes the curveballs life gives her and turns them into home runs. Despite the odds stacked against her, she was able to move past her failures and do what was necessary to build a better future. The world can be a tough place to navigate, and it takes serious determination—and faith—to be successful. Lindsay had the first trait all along, and once she discovered the second, she found the strength to make a good life for herself and her daughter.

If you'd like to stop in and see what I've been up to, you'll find me online at miaross.com, Facebook, Twitter and Goodreads. While you're there, send me a message in your favorite format. I'd love to hear from you!

Mia Ross

COMING NEXT MONTH FROM
Love Inspired®

Available February 20, 2018

AN UNEXPECTED AMISH ROMANCE
The Amish Bachelors • by Patricia Davids

Mourning a broken engagement, Helen Zook flees to Bowman's Crossing. There she finds herself clashing with her new boss, Mark Bowman. Sparks fly. But with Mark soon returning to his hometown, is there any chance at a future together?

COURTING THE AMISH DOCTOR
Prodigal Daughters • by Mary Davis

Single doctor Kathleen Yoder returns to her Amish community knowing acceptance of her profession won't come easy—but at least she has the charming Noah Lambright on her side. Even as Kathleen comes to depend on Noah's support, she knows an Amish husband would never accept a doctor wife. Could Noah be the exception?

A FAMILY FOR EASTER
Rescue River • by Lee Tobin McClain

When Fiona Farmingham offers to rent her carriage house to single dad Eduardo Delgado after a fire at his home, he accepts. Having failed his deceased wife, he plans to keep their relationship strictly professional. But six rambunctious kids, one wily dog and Fiona's kind heart soon have him falling for the pretty widow.

HER ALASKAN COWBOY
Alaskan Grooms • by Belle Calhoune

Honor Prescott is shocked former sweetheart Joshua Ransom is back in Love, Alaska—and that he's selling his grandfather's ranch to a developer! As a wildlife conservationist, Honor is determined to stop that sale. But when the secret behind Joshua's departure is revealed, can she prevent herself from falling for the Alaskan cowboy once again?

FINALLY A BRIDE
Willow's Haven • by Renee Andrews

Disappointed by love, veterinarian Haley Calhoun decides her practice and her Adopt-an-Animal program are enough. Until she discovers the handsome widower who showed up at her clinic with an orphaned boy and his puppy will be her point of contact for the adoption program. Will working together give both of them a second chance at forever?

THEIR SECRET BABY BOND
Family Blessings • by Stephanie Dees

Mom-to-be Wynn Sheehan left her dream job in Washington, DC, after her heart was broken. When she becomes the caregiver for Latham Grant's grandfather, she's drawn once again to her long-ago boyfriend. But with her life now in shambles, is her happily-ever-after out of reach for good?

LOOK FOR THESE AND OTHER LOVE INSPIRED BOOKS WHEREVER BOOKS ARE SOLD, INCLUDING MOST BOOKSTORES, SUPERMARKETS, DISCOUNT STORES AND DRUGSTORES.

LICNM0218

Get 2 Free Books,

Plus 2 Free Gifts—
just for trying the Reader Service!

SPECIAL EXCERPT FROM

*Fresh off heartbreak, will Helen Zook find peace in
Bowmans Corner...and love again with her new boss?*

Read on for a sneak preview of
AN UNEXPECTED AMISH ROMANCE
by **Patricia Davids**,
available March 2018 from Love Inspired!

Mark Bowman lifted his straw hat off his face and sat
up with a disgruntled sigh. Trying to sleep on a bus was
hard enough, but the sound of muffled weeping coming
from the seat behind him was making it impossible.
He turned to look over his shoulder. The culprit was
an Amish woman with her face buried in a large white
handkerchief. She was alone.

"*Frauline*, are you all right?"

She glanced up and then turned her face to the window.
"I'm fine."

It was dark outside. There was nothing to see except
the occasional lights from the farms they passed. She
dabbed her eyes and sniffled. She was a lovely woman.
Her pale blond hair was tucked neatly beneath a gauzy,
heart-shaped white *kapp*. He didn't recognize the style
and wondered where she was from. "You don't sound
fine."

"Maybe not yet, but I will be."

The defiance in her tone took him by surprise and
reminded him of his six-year-old sister when she didn't
get her way. Experience had taught him the best way to

LIEXP0218

stop his sister's tears was to distract her. "I don't care much for bus rides. Makes me queasy in the stomach. How about you?"

"It doesn't bother me."

"Where are you headed?"

"To visit family." The woman's clipped reply said she wasn't interested in talking about it. He should have let it go at that, but he didn't.

"Then someone in your family must be ill. Or perhaps you are on your way to a funeral."

She frowned at him. "Why do you say that?"

"It's a reasonable assumption. You'd hardly be crying if you were on your way to a wedding."

Tears welled up in her eyes and spilled down her cheeks. With a strangled cry, she scrambled out of her seat and moved to one at the rear of the bus, effectively ending their conversation.

Confused, he stared at her. Somehow he'd made things worse, and he had no idea what he'd said that upset her so. He shook his head in bewilderment.

Don't miss
AN UNEXPECTED AMISH ROMANCE
by Patricia Davids,
available March 2018 wherever
Love Inspired® books and ebooks are sold.

www.LoveInspired.com

Looking for inspiration in tales
of hope, faith and heartfelt romance?

Check out **Love Inspired**® and
Love Inspired® **Suspense** books!

New books available every month!

CONNECT WITH US AT:

Harlequin.com/Community

Facebook.com/HarlequinBooks

Twitter.com/HarlequinBooks

Instagram.com/HarlequinBooks

Pinterest.com/HarlequinBooks

ReaderService.com

Love Inspired®

LIGENRE2018

SPECIAL EXCERPT FROM

Love Inspired
SUSPENSE

*After FBI special agent Adam Whitfield's ex-wife,
Charlotte Murray, is nearly killed when she stops
an abduction, the serial killer Adam's been hunting
turns his focus on her for getting in his way.
Now Adam has two missions: bring the murderer
to justice...and save Charlotte.*

*Read on for a sneak preview of **Shirlee McCoy**'s,
NIGHT STALKER, the exciting first book of the
miniseries **FBI: SPECIAL CRIMES UNIT**,
available March 2018 from Love Inspired Suspense!*

"Charlotte, I'm sure you know exactly why leaving the hospital isn't a good idea."

"The Night Stalker doesn't know who I am. He doesn't know where I live, and as far as law enforcement can tell, he left town and hasn't returned."

"Law enforcement has no idea who he is or where he lives."

"Wren said the Night Stalker probably hunted for his victims far away from home. If that's the case, he doesn't live anywhere near here," she commented.

"He changed his MO when he went after Bethany. He's always taken women from large hospitals. This time, it's different."

"That doesn't mean he lives close by."

"It doesn't mean that he doesn't," Adam pointed out.

"I don't know what you want me to say, Adam."

"I want you to say that you're going to follow the team's plan."

"What plan? The one where I get on a private jet and travel to an unknown destination?"

"Yes."

"Were you part of making it? Is that why you want me to agree to it?"

"You know I'm on leave," he said. "I have nothing to do with the plans that are made."

"I'm sure you'd like to be part of the decision-making process. You can go back to Boston and back to work," she replied, and felt like an ogre for it. Adam had been nothing but kind, and she'd done nothing but try to push him away.

"No. I can't. Not until I know you're safe."

"I don't need you to keep me safe," she murmured, but her heart wasn't in the words. They sounded hollow and sad and a little lonely.

"I didn't say you did. I said I need to know you are. I still care about you, Charlotte. That has never changed. For the record," he said, "I don't approve."

"Your disapproval is noted."

"But you're leaving anyway?"

"Yes."

"I'll get a wheelchair. I'll be right back."

Minutes later, he wheeled the chair in. "River and Wren are accompanying us to your place. They'll be staying there until you make a decision about protective custody."

"I don't remember agreeing to that."

"You didn't."

She could have argued.

She could have listed a dozen reasons why she didn't want or need federal officers in her house. Except that she wasn't 100 percent sure she didn't need them.

If the Night Stalker really did live somewhere nearby, he might be someone she knew, someone who'd recognized her.

Someone who wanted to make sure that she didn't recognize him.

Don't miss
NIGHT STALKER by Shirlee McCoy,
available March 2018 wherever
Love Inspired® Suspense books and ebooks are sold.

www.LoveInspired.com

Inspirational Romance to Warm Your Heart and Soul

Join our social communities to connect with other readers who share your love!

Sign up for the Love Inspired newsletter at **www.LoveInspired.com** to be the first to find out about upcoming titles, special promotions and exclusive content.

CONNECT WITH US AT:

Harlequin.com/Community

 Facebook.com/LoveInspiredBooks

 Twitter.com/LoveInspiredBks

DAVID GROSSMAN

Falling Out
of Time

TRANSLATED FROM THE HEBREW BY
Jessica Cohen

VINTAGE BOOKS
London

First published in the United States by Alfred A. Knopf,
a division of Random House, Inc., New York

First published in Great Britain in 2014 by
Jonathan Cape

Vintage
20 Vauxhall Bridge Road,
London SW1V 2SA

www.vintage-books.co.uk

 Penguin
Random House
UK

A Penguin Random House Company

global.penguinrandomhouse.com

A CIP catalogue record for this book
is available from the British Library

ISBN 9780099583721

Penguin Random House supports the Forest Stewardship
Council (FSC®), the leading international forest certification
organisation. Our books carrying the FSC® label are printed on
FSC®-certified paper. FSC® is the only forest certification scheme
endorsed by the leading environmental organisations, including
Greenpeace. Our paper procurement policy can be
found at www.randomhouse.co.uk/environment

Printed and bound in Great Britain by Clays Ltd, St Ives plc

Falling Out of Time